THE GREAT WAR
SYNDICATE

FRANK R. STOCKTON

1st WORLD
LIBRARY
Literary Society

The Great War Syndicate

Frank R. Stockton

© 1st World Library, 2007
PO Box 2211
Fairfield, IA 52556
www.1stworldlibrary.com
First Edition

LCCN: 2007930834

Softcover ISBN: 978-1-4218-4822-8
Hardcover ISBN: 978-1-4218-4725-2
eBook ISBN: 978-1-4218-4919-5

Purchase *"The Great War Syndicate"*
as a traditional bound book at:
www.1stWorldLibrary.com/purchase.asp?ISBN=978-1-4218-4822-8

1st World Library is a literary, educational organization
dedicated to:

- Creating a free internet library of downloadable ebooks

- Hosting writing competitions and offering book publishing
scholarships.

Interested in more 1st World Library books? contact:
literacy@1stworldlibrary.com
Check us out at: www.1stworldlibrary.com

1st World Library Literary Society

Giving Back to the World

"If you want to work on the core problem, it's early school literacy."

- James Barksdale, former CEO of Netscape

"No skill is more crucial to the future of a child, or to a democratic and prosperous society, than literacy."

- Los Angeles Times

"Literacy... means far more than learning how to read and write... The aim is to transmit... knowledge and promote social participation."

- UNESCO

"Literacy is not a luxury, it is a right and a responsibility. If our world is to meet the challenges of the twenty-first century we must harness the energy and creativity of all our citizens."

- President Bill Clinton

"Parents should be encouraged to read to their children, and teachers should be equipped with all available techniques for teaching literacy, so the varying needs and capacities of individual kids can be taken into account."

- Hugh Mackay

THE GREAT WAR SYNDICATE

In the spring of a certain year, not far from the close of the nineteenth century, when the political relations between the United States and Great Britain became so strained that careful observers on both sides of the Atlantic were forced to the belief that a serious break in these relations might be looked for at any time, the fishing schooner Eliza Drum sailed from a port in Maine for the banks of Newfoundland.

It was in this year that a new system of protection for American fishing vessels had been adopted in Washington. Every fleet of these vessels was accompanied by one or more United States cruisers, which remained on the fishing grounds, not only for the purpose of warning American craft who might approach too near the three-mile limit, but also to overlook the action of the British naval vessels on the coast, and to interfere, at least by protest, with such seizures of American fishing boats as might appear to be unjust. In the opinion of all persons of sober judgment, there was nothing in the condition of affairs at this time so dangerous to the peace of the two countries as the presence of these American cruisers in the fishing waters.

The Eliza Drum was late in her arrival on the fishing grounds, and having, under orders from Washington, reported to the commander of the Lennehaha, the United States vessel in charge at that place, her captain and crew went vigorously to work to make up for lost time. They worked so vigorously, and with eyes so single to the catching of fish, that on the morning of the day after their arrival, they were hauling up cod at a point which, according to the nationality of the calculator, might be two and three-quarters or three and one-quarter miles from the Canadian coast.

In consequence of this inattention to the apparent extent of the marine mile, the Eliza Drum, a little before noon, was overhauled and seized by the British cruiser, Dog Star. A few miles away the Lennehaha had perceived the dangerous position of the Eliza Drum, and had started toward her to warn her to take a less doubtful position. But before she arrived the capture had taken place. When he reached the spot where the Eliza Drum had been fishing, the commander of the Lennehaha made an observation of the distance from the shore, and calculated it to be more than three miles. When he sent an officer in a boat to the Dog Star to state the result of his computations, the captain of the British vessel replied that he was satisfied the distance was less than three miles, and that he was now about to take the Eliza Drum into port.

On receiving this information, the commander of the Lennehaha steamed closer to the Dog Star, and informed her captain, by means of a speaking-trumpet, that if he took the Eliza Drum into a Canadian port, he would first have to sail over his ship. To this the captain of the Dog Star replied that he did not in the least object to sail over the Lennehaha, and proceeded to put a prize crew on board the fishing vessel.

At this juncture the captain of the Eliza Drum ran up a large American flag; in five minutes afterward the captain of the prize crew hauled it down; in less than ten minutes after this the Lennehaha and the Dog Star were blazing at each other with their bow guns. The spark had been struck.

Frank R. Stockton

The contest was not a long one. The Dog Star was of much greater tonnage and heavier armament than her antagonist, and early in the afternoon she steamed for St. John's, taking with her as prizes both the Eliza Drum and the Lennehaha.

All that night, at every point in the United States which was reached by telegraph, there burned a smothered fire; and the next morning, when the regular and extra editions of the newspapers were poured out upon the land, the fire burst into a roaring blaze. From lakes to gulf, from ocean to ocean, on mountain and plain, in city and prairie, it roared and blazed. Parties, sections, politics, were all forgotten. Every American formed part of an electric system; the same fire flashed into every soul. No matter what might be thought on the morrow, or in the coming days which might bring better under-standing, this day the unreasoning fire blazed and roared.

With morning newspapers in their hands, men rushed from the breakfast-tables into the streets to meet their fellow-men. What was it that they should do?

Detailed accounts of the affair came rapidly, but there was nothing in them to quiet the national indignation; the American flag had been hauled down by Englishmen, an American naval vessel had been fired into and captured; that was enough! No matter whether the Eliza Drum was within the three-mile limit or not! No matter which vessel fired first! If it were the Lennehaha, the more honour to her; she ought to have done it! From platform, pulpit, stump, and editorial office came one vehement, passionate shout directed toward Washington.

Congress was in session, and in its halls the fire roared louder and blazed higher than on mountain or plain, in city or prairie. No member of the Government, from President to page, ventured to oppose the tempestuous demands of the people. The day for argument upon the exciting question had been a long weary one, and it had gone by in less than a week the great shout of the people was answered by a declaration of war against Great Britain.

When this had been done, those who demanded war breathed easier, but those who must direct the war breathed harder.

It was indeed a time for hard breathing, but the great mass of the people perceived no reason why this should be. Money there was in vast abundance. In every State well-drilled men, by thousands, stood ready for the word to march, and the military experience and knowledge given by a great war was yet strong upon the nation.

To the people at large the plan of the war appeared a very obvious and a very simple one. Canada had given the offence, Canada should be made to pay the penalty. In a very short time, one hundred thousand, two hundred thousand, five hundred thousand men, if necessary, could be made ready for the invasion of Canada. From platform, pulpit, stump, and editorial office came the cry: "On to Canada!"

At the seat of Government, however, the plan of the war did not appear so obvious, so simple. Throwing a great army into Canada was all well enough, and that army would probably do well enough; but the question which produced hard breathing in the executive branch of the Government was the immediate protection of the sea-coast, Atlantic, Gulf, and even Pacific.

In a storm of national indignation war had been declared against a power which at this period of her history had brought up her naval forces to a point double in strength to that of any other country in the world. And this war had been declared by a nation which, comparatively speaking, possessed no naval strength at all.

Frank R. Stockton

For some years the United States navy had been steadily improving, but this improvement was not sufficient to make it worthy of reliance at this crisis. As has been said, there was money enough, and every ship-yard in the country could be set to work to build ironclad men-of-war: but it takes a long time to build ships, and England's navy was afloat. It was theBritish keel that America had to fear.

By means of the continental cables it was known that many of the largest mail vessels of the British transatlantic lines, which had been withdrawn upon the declaration of war, were preparing in British ports to transport troops to Canada. It was not impossible that these great steamers might land an army in Canada before an American army could be organized and marched to that province. It might be that the United States would be forced to defend her borders, instead of invading those of the enemy.

In every fort and navy-yard all was activity; the hammering of iron went on by day and by night; but what was to be done when the great ironclads of England hammered upon our defences? How long would it be before the American flag would be seen no more upon the high seas?

It is not surprising that the Government found its position one of perilous responsibility. A wrathful nation expected of it more than it could perform.

All over the country, however, there were thoughtful men, not connected with the Government, who saw the perilous features of the situation; and day by day these grew less afraid of being considered traitors, and more willing to declare their convictions of the country's danger. Despite the continuance of the national enthusiasm, doubts, perplexities, and fears began to show themselves.

In the States bordering upon Canada a reactionary feeling

became evident. Unless the United States navy could prevent England from rapidly pouring into Canada, not only her own troops, but perhaps those of allied nations, these Northern States might become the scene of warfare, and whatever the issue of the contest, their lands might be ravished, their people suffer.

From many quarters urgent demands were now pressed upon the Government. From the interior there were clamours for troops to be massed on the Northern frontier, and from the seaboard cities there came a cry for ships that were worthy to be called men-of-war,—ships to defend the harbours and bays, ships to repel an invasion by sea. Suggestions were innumerable. There was no time to build, it was urged; the Government could call upon friendly nations. But wise men smiled sadly at these suggestions; it was difficult to find a nation desirous of a war with England.

In the midst of the enthusiasms, the fears, and the suggestions, came reports of the capture of American merchantmen by fast British cruisers. These reports made the American people more furious, the American Government more anxious.

Almost from the beginning of this period of national turmoil, a party of gentlemen met daily in one of the large rooms in a hotel in New York. At first there were eleven of these men, all from the great Atlantic cities, but their number increased by arrivals from other parts of the country, until at last they, numbered twenty-three. These gentlemen were all great capitalists, and accustomed to occupying themselves with great enterprises. By day and by night they met together with closed doors, until they had matured the scheme which they had been considering. As soon as this work was done, a committee was sent to Washington, to submit a plan to the Government.

Frank R. Stockton

These twenty-three men had formed themselves into a Syndicate, with the object of taking entire charge of the war between the United States and Great Britain.

This proposition was an astounding one, but the Government was obliged to treat it with respectful consideration. The men who offered it were a power in the land,—a power which no government could afford to disregard.

The plan of the Syndicate was comprehensive, direct, and simple. It offered to assume the entire control and expense of the war, and to effect a satisfactory peace within one year. As a guarantee that this contract would be properly performed, an immense sum of money would be deposited in the Treasury at Washington. Should the Syndicate be unsuccessful, this sum would be forfeited, and it would receive no pay for anything it had done.

The sum to be paid by the Government to the Syndicate, should it bring the war to a satisfactory conclusion, would depend upon the duration of hostilities. That is to say, that as the shorter the duration of the war, the greater would be the benefit to the country, therefore, the larger must be the pay to the Syndicate. According to the proposed contract, the Syndicate would receive, if the war should continue for a year, one-quarter the sum stipulated to be paid if peace should be declared in three months.

If at any time during the conduct of the war by the Syndicate an American seaport should be taken by the enemy, or a British force landed on any point of the seacoast, the contract should be considered at an end, and security and payment forfeited. If any point on the northern boundary of the United States should be taken and occupied by the enemy, one million dollars of the deposited security should be forfeited for every such occupation, but the contract should continue.

It was stipulated that the land and naval forces of the United States should remain under the entire control of the Government, but should be maintained as a defensive force, and not brought into action unless any failure on the part of the Syndicate should render such action necessary.

The state of feeling in governmental circles, and the evidences of alarm and distrust which were becoming apparent in Congress and among the people, exerted an important influence in favour of the Syndicate. The Government caught at its proposition, not as if it were a straw, but as if it were a life-raft. The men who offered to relieve the executive departments of their perilous responsibilities were men of great ability, prominent positions, and vast resources, whose vast enterprises had already made them known all over the globe. Such men were not likely to jeopardize their reputations and fortunes in a case like this, unless they had well-founded reasons for believing that they would be successful. Even the largest amount stipulated to be paid them in case of success would be less than the ordinary estimates for the military and naval operations which had been anticipated; and in case of failure, the amount forfeited would go far to repair the losses which might be sustained by the citizens of the various States.

At all events, should the Syndicate be allowed to take immediate control of the war, there would be time to put the army and navy, especially the latter, in better condition to carry on the contest in case of the failure of the Syndicate. Organization and construction might still go on, and, should it be necessary, the army and navy could step into the contest fresh and well prepared.

All branches of the Government united in accepting the offer of the Syndicate. The contract was signed, and the world waited to see what would happen next.

Frank R. Stockton

The influence which for years had been exerted by the interests controlled by the men composing the Syndicate, had its effect in producing a popular confidence in the power of the members of the Syndicate to conduct a war as successfully as they had conducted other gigantic enterprises. Therefore, although predictions of disaster came from many quarters, the American public appeared willing to wait with but moderate impatience for the result of this novel undertaking.

The Government now proceeded to mass troops at important points on the northern frontier; forts were supplied with men and armaments, all coast defences were put in the best possible condition, the navy was stationed at important ports, and work at the ship-yards went on. But without reference to all this, the work of the Syndicate immediately began.

This body of men were of various politics and of various pursuits in life. But politics were no more regarded in the work they had undertaken than they would have been in the purchase of land or of railroad iron. No manifestoes of motives and intentions were issued to the public. The Syndicate simply went to work. There could be no doubt that early success would be a direct profit to it, but there could also be no doubt that its success would be a vast benefit and profit, not only to the business enterprises in which these men were severally engaged, but to the business of the whole country. To save the United States from a dragging war, and to save themselves from the effects of it, were the prompting motives for the formation of the Syndicate.

Without hesitation, the Syndicate determined that the war in which it was about to engage should be one of defence by means of offence. Such a war must necessarily be quick and effective; and with all the force of their fortunes, their minds, and their bodies, its members went to work to wage this war quickly and effectively.

All known inventions and improvements in the art of war had been thoroughly considered by the Syndicate, and by the eminent specialists whom it had enlisted in its service. Certain recently perfected engines of war, novel in nature, were the exclusive property of the Syndicate. It was known, or surmised, in certain quarters that the Syndicate had secured possession of important warlike inventions; but what they were and how they acted was a secret carefully guarded and protected.

The first step of the Syndicate was to purchase from the United States Government ten war-vessels. These were of medium size and in good condition, but they were of an old-fashioned type, and it had not been considered expedient to put them in commission. This action caused surprise and disappointment in many quarters. It had been supposed that the Syndicate, through its agents scattered all over the world, would immediately acquire, by purchase or lease, a fleet of fine ironclads culled from various maritime powers. But the Syndicate having no intention of involving, or attempting to involve, other countries in this quarrel, paid no attention to public opinion, and went to work in its own way.

Its vessels, eight of which were on the Atlantic coast and two on the Pacific, were rapidly prepared for the peculiar service in which they were to be engaged. The resources of the Syndicate were great, and in a very short time several of their vessels, already heavily plated with steel, were furnished with an additional outside armour, formed of strips of elastic steel, each reaching from the gunwales nearly to the surface of the water. These strips, about a foot wide, and placed an inch or two apart, were each backed by several powerful air-buffers, so that a ball striking one or more of them would be deprived of much of its momentum. The experiments upon the steel spring and buffers adopted by the Syndicate showed that the force of the heaviest cannonading was almost deadened by the powerful elasticity of this armour.

Frank R. Stockton

The armament of each vessel consisted of but one gun, of large calibre, placed on the forward deck, and protected by a bomb-proof covering. Each vessel was manned by a captain and crew from the merchant service, from whom no warlike duties were expected. The fighting operations were in charge of a small body of men, composed of two or three scientific specialists, and some practical gunners and their assistants. A few bomb-proof canopies and a curved steel deck completed the defences of the vessel.

Besides equipping this little navy, the Syndicate set about the construction of certain sea-going vessels of an extraordinary kind. So great were the facilities at its command, and so thorough and complete its methods, that ten or a dozen ship-yards and foundries were set to work simultaneously to build one of these ships. In a marvellously short time the Syndicate possessed several of them ready for action.

These vessels became technically known as "crabs." They were not large, and the only part of them which projected above the water was the middle of an elliptical deck, slightly convex, and heavily mailed with ribs of steel. These vessels were fitted with electric engines of extraordinary power, and were capable of great speed. At their bows, fully protected by the overhanging deck, was the machinery by which their peculiar work was to be accomplished. The Syndicate intended to confine itself to marine operations, and for the present it was contented with these two classes of vessels.

The armament for each of the large vessels, as has been said before, consisted of a single gun of long range, and the ammunition was confined entirely to a new style of projectile, which had never yet been used in warfare. The material and construction of this projectile were known only to three members of the Syndicate, who had invented and perfected it, and it was on account of their possession of this secret that they had been invited to join that body.

This projectile was not, in the ordinary sense of the word, an explosive, and was named by its inventors, "The Instantaneous Motor." It was discharged from an ordinary cannon, but no gunpowder or other explosive compound was used to propel it. The bomb possessed, in itself the necessary power of propulsion, and the gun was used merely to give it the proper direction.

These bombs were cylindrical in form, and pointed at the outer end. They were filled with hundreds of small tubes, each radiating outward from a central line. Those in the middle third of the bomb pointed directly outward, while those in its front portion were inclined forward at a slight angle, and those in the rear portion backward at the same angle. One tube at the end of the bomb, and pointing directly backward, furnished the motive power.

Each of these tubes could exert a force sufficient to move an ordinary train of passenger cars one mile, and this power could be exerted instantaneously, so that the difference in time in the starting of a train at one end of the mile and its arrival at the other would not be appreciable. The difference in concussionary force between a train moving at the rate of a mile in two minutes, or even one minute, and another train which moves a mile in an instant, can easily be imagined.

In these bombs, those tubes which might direct their powers downward or laterally upon the earth were capable of instantaneously propelling every portion of solid ground or rock to a distance of two or three hundred yards, while the particles of objects on the surface of the earth were instantaneously removed to a far greater distance. The tube which propelled the bomb was of a force graduated according to circumstances, and it would carry a bomb to as great a distance as accurate observation for purposes of aim could be made. Its force was brought into action while in the cannon by means of electricity while the same effect was produced in the other

Frank R. Stockton

tubes by the concussion of the steel head against the object aimed at.

What gave the tubes their power was the jealously guarded secret.

The method of aiming was as novel as the bomb itself. In this process nothing depended on the eyesight of the gunner; the personal equation was entirely eliminated. The gun was so mounted that its direction was accurately indicated by graduated scales; there was an instrument which was acted upon by the dip, rise, or roll of the vessel, and which showed at any moment the position of the gun with reference to the plane of the sea-surface.

Before the discharge of the cannon an observation was taken by one of the scientific men, which accurately determined the distance to the object to be aimed at, and reference to a carefully prepared mathematical table showed to what points on the graduated scales the gun should be adjusted, and the instant that the that the muzzle of the cannon was in the position that it was when the observation was taken, a button was touched and the bomb was instantaneously placed on the spot aimed at. The exactness with which the propelling force of the bomb could be determined was an important factor in this method of aiming.

As soon as three of the spring-armoured vessels and five "crabs" were completed, the Syndicate felt itself ready to begin operations. It was indeed time. The seas had been covered with American and British merchantmen hastening homeward, or to friendly ports, before the actual commencement of hostilities. But all had not been fortunate enough to reach safety within the limits of time allowed, and several American merchantmen had been already captured by fast British cruisers.

The members of the Syndicate well understood that if a war was to be carried on as they desired, they must strike the first real blow. Comparatively speaking, a very short time had elapsed since the declaration of war, and the opportunity to take the initiative was still open.

It was in order to take this initiative that, in the early hours of a July morning, two of the Syndicate's armoured vessels, each accompanied by a crab, steamed out of a New England port, and headed for the point on the Canadian coast where it had been decided to open the campaign.

The vessels of the Syndicate had no individual names. The spring-armoured ships were termed "repellers," and were numbered, and the crabs were known by the letters of the alphabet. Each repeller was in charge of a Director of Naval Operations; and the whole naval force of the Syndicate was under the command of a Director-in-chief. On this momentous occasion this officer was on board of Repeller No. 1, and commanded the little fleet.

The repellers had never been vessels of great speed, and their present armour of steel strips, the lower portion of which was frequently under water, considerably retarded their progress; but each of them was taken in tow by one of the swift and powerful crabs, and with this assistance they made very good time, reaching their destination on the morning of the second day.

It was on a breezy day, with a cloudy sky, and the sea moderately smooth, that the little fleet of the Syndicate lay to off the harbour of one of the principal Canadian seaports. About five miles away the headlands on either side of the mouth of the harbour could be plainly seen. It had been decided that Repeller No. 1 should begin operations. Accordingly, that vessel steamed about a mile nearer the harbour, accompanied by Crab A. The other repeller and crab remained in their first position, ready to act in case they should be needed.

The approach of two vessels, evidently men-of-war, and carrying the American flag, was perceived from the forts and redoubts at the mouth of the harbour, and the news quickly spread to the city and to the vessels in port. Intense excitement ensued on land and water, among the citizens of the place as well as its defenders. Every man who had a post of duty was instantly at it; and in less than half an hour the British man-of-war Scarabaeus, which had been lying at anchor a short distance outside the harbour, came steaming out to meet the enemy. There were other naval vessels in port, but they required more time to be put in readiness for action.

As soon as the approach of Scarabaeus was perceived by Repeller No. 1, a boat bearing a white flag was lowered from that vessel and was rapidly rowed toward the British ship. When the latter saw the boat coming she lay to, and waited its arrival. A note was delivered to the captain of the Scarabaeus, in which it was stated that the Syndicate, which had undertaken on the part of the United States the conduct of the war between that country and Great Britain, was now prepared to demand the surrender of this city with its forts and defences and all vessels within its harbour, and, as a first step, the immediate surrender of the vessel to the commander of which this note was delivered.

The overwhelming effrontery of this demand caused the commander of the Scarabaeus to doubt whether he had to deal with a raving lunatic or a blustering fool; but he informed the person in charge of the flag-of-truce boat, that he would give him fifteen minutes in which to get back to his vessel, and that he would then open fire upon that craft.

The men who rowed the little boat were not men-of-war's men, and were unaccustomed to duties of this kind. In eight minutes they had reached their vessel, and were safe on board.

Just seven minutes afterward the first shot came from the Scarabaeus. It passed over Repeller No. 1, and that vessel, instead of replying, immediately steamed nearer her adversary. The Director-in-chief desired to determine the effect of an active cannonade upon the new armour, and therefore ordered the vessel placed in such a position that the Englishman might have the best opportunity for using it as a target.

The Scarabaeus lost no time in availing herself of the facilities offered. She was a large and powerful ship, with a heavy armament; and, soon getting the range of the Syndicate's vessel, she hurled ball after ball upon her striped side. Repeller No. 1 made no reply, but quietly submitted to the terrible bombardment. Some of the great shot jarred her from bow to stern, but not one of them broke a steel spring, nor penetrated the heavy inside plates.

After half an hour of this, work the Director-in- chief became satisfied that the new armour had well acquitted itself in the severe trial to which it had been subjected. Some of the air-buffers had been disabled, probably on account of faults in their construction, but these could readily be replaced, and no further injury had been done the vessel. It was not necessary, therefore, to continue the experiment any longer, and besides, there was danger that the Englishman, perceiving that his antagonist did not appear to be affected by his fire, would approach closer and endeavour to ram her. This was to be avoided, for the Scarabaeus was a much larger vessel than Repeller No. 1, and able to run into the latter and sink her by mere preponderance of weight.

It was therefore decided to now test the powers of the crabs. Signals were made from Repeller No. 1 to Crab A, which had been lying with the larger vessel between it and the enemy. These signals were made by jets of dense black smoke, which were ejected from a small pipe on the repeller. These slender columns of smoke preserved their cylindrical forms for some moments, and were visible at a great distance by day or night, being illumined in the latter case by electric light. The length and frequency of these jets were regulated by an instrument in the Director's room. Thus, by means of long and short puffs, with the proper use of intervals, a message could be projected into the air as a telegraphic instrument would mark it upon paper.

In this manner Crab A was ordered to immediately proceed to the attack of the Scarabaeus. The almost submerged vessel steamed rapidly from behind her consort, and made for the British man-of-war.

When the latter vessel perceived the approach of this turtle-backed object, squirting little jets of black smoke as she replied to the orders from the repeller, there was great amazement on board. The crab had not been seen before, but as it came rapidly on there was no time for curiosity or discussion, and several heavy guns were brought to bear upon it. It was difficult to hit a rapidly moving flat object scarcely above the surface of the water; and although several shot struck the crab, they glanced off without in the least interfering with its progress.

Crab A soon came so near the Scarabaeus that it was impossible to depress the guns of the latter so as to strike her. The great vessel was, therefore, headed toward its assailant, and under a full head of steam dashed directly at it to run it down. But the crab could turn as upon a pivot, and shooting to one side allowed the surging man-of-war to pass it.

Perceiving instantly that it would be difficult to strike this nimble and almost submerged adversary, the commander of the Scarabaeus thought it well to let it alone for the present, and to bear down with all speed upon the repeller. But it was easier to hit the crab than to leave it behind. It was capable of great speed, and, following the British vessel, it quickly came up with her.

The course of the Scarabaeus was instantly changed, and every effort was made to get the vessel into a position to run down the crab. But this was not easy for so large a ship, and Crab A seemed to have no difficulty in keeping close to her stern.

Several machine-guns, especially adopted for firing at torpedo-boats or any hostile craft which might be discovered close to a vessel, were now brought to bear upon the crab, and ball after ball was hurled at her. Some of these struck, but glanced off without penetrating her tough armour.

These manoeuvres had not continued long, when the crew of the crab was ready to bring into action the peculiar apparatus of that peculiar craft. An enormous pair of iron forceps, each massive limb of which measured twelve feet or more in length, was run out in front of the crab at a depth of six or eight feet below the surface. These forceps were acted upon by an electric engine of immense power, by which they could be shut, opened, projected, withdrawn, or turned and twisted.

The crab darted forward, and in the next instant the great teeth of her pincers were fastened with a tremendous grip upon the rudder and rudder-post of the Scarabaeus.

Then followed a sudden twist, which sent a thrill through both vessels; a crash; a backward jerk; the snapping of a chain; and in a moment the great rudder, with half of the rudder-post attached, was torn from the vessel, and as the forceps opened it dropped to leeward and hung dangling by

Frank R. Stockton

one chain.

Again the forceps opened wide; again there was a rush; and this time the huge jaws closed upon the rapidly revolving screw-propeller. There was a tremendous crash, and the small but massive crab turned over so far that for an instant one of its sides was plainly visible above the water. The blades of the propeller were crushed and shivered; those parts of the steamer's engines connecting with the propeller-shaft were snapped and rent apart, while the propeller-shaft itself was broken by the violent stoppage.

The crab, which had quickly righted, now backed, still holding the crushed propeller in its iron grasp, and as it moved away from the Scarabaeus, it extracted about forty feet of its propeller-shaft; then, opening its massive jaws, it allowed the useless mass of iron to drop to the bottom of the sea.

Every man on board the Scarabaeus was wild with amazement and excitement. Few could comprehend what had happened, but this very quickly became evident. So far as motive power was concerned, the Scarabaeus was totally, disabled. She could not direct her course, for her rudder was gone, her propeller was gone, her engines were useless, and she could do no more than float as wind or tide might move her. Moreover, there was a jagged hole in her stern where the shaft had been, and through this the water was pouring into the vessel. As a man-of-war the Scarabaeus was worthless.

Orders now came fast from Repeller No. 1, which had moved nearer to the scene of conflict. It was to be supposed that the disabled ship was properly furnished with bulkheads, so that the water would penetrate no farther than the stern compartment, and that, therefore, she was in no danger of sinking. Crab A was ordered to make fast to the bow of the Scarabaeus, and tow her toward two men-of-war who were rapidly approaching from the harbour.

This proceeding astonished the commander and officers of the Scarabaeus almost as much as the extraordinary attack which had been made upon their ship. They had expected a demand to surrender and haul down their flag; but the Director-in-chief on board Repeller No. 1 was of the opinion that with her propeller extracted it mattered little what flag she flew. His work with the Scarabaeus was over; for it had been ordered by the Syndicate that its vessels should not encumber themselves with prizes.

Towed by the powerful crab, which apparently had no fear that its disabled adversary might fire upon it, the Scarabaeus moved toward the harbour, and when it had come within a quarter of a mile of the foremost British vessel, Crab A cast off and steamed back to Repeller No. 1.

The other English vessels soon came up, and each lay to and sent a boat to the Scarabaeus. After half an hour's consultation, in which the amazement of those on board the damaged vessel was communicated to the officers and crews of her two consorts, it was determined that the smaller of these should tow the disabled ship into port, while the other one, in company with a man-of-war just coming out of the harbour, should make an attack upon Repeller No. 1.

It had been plainly proved that ordinary shot and shell had no effect upon this craft; but it had not been proved that she could withstand the rams of powerful ironclads. If this vessel, that apparently carried no guns, or, at least, had used none, could be crushed, capsized, sunk, or in any way put out of the fight, it was probable that the dangerous submerged nautical machine would not care to remain in these waters. If it remained it must be destroyed by torpedoes.

Signals were exchanged between the two English vessels, and in a very short time they were steaming toward the repeller. It was a dangerous thing for two vessels of their size

Frank R. Stockton

to come close enough together for both to ram an enemy at the same time, but it was determined to take the risks and do this, if possible; for the destruction of the repeller was obviously the first duty in hand.

As the two men-of-war rapidly approached Repeller No. 1, they kept up a steady fire upon her; for if in this way they could damage her, the easier would be their task. With a firm reliance upon the efficacy of the steel-spring armour, the Director-in-chief felt no fear of the enemy's shot and shell; but he was not at all willing that his vessel should be rammed, for the consequences would probably be disastrous. Accordingly he did not wait for the approach of the two vessels, but steering seaward, he signalled for the other crab.

When Crab B made its appearance, puffing its little black jets of smoke, as it answered the signals of the Director-in-chief, the commanders of the two British vessels were surprised. They had imagined that there was only one of these strange and terrible enemies, and had supposed that she would be afraid to make her peculiar attack upon one of them, because while doing so she would expose herself to the danger of being run down by the other. But the presence of two of these almost submerged engines of destruction entirely changed the situation.

But the commanders of the British ships were brave men. They had started to run down the strangely armoured American craft, and run her down they would, if they could. They put on more steam, and went ahead at greater speed. In such a furious onslaught the crabs might not dare to attack them.

But they did not understand the nature nor the powers of these enemies. In less than twenty minutes Crab A had laid hold of one of the men-of-war, and Crab B of the other. The rudders of both were shattered and torn away; and while the blades of one propeller were crushed to pieces, the other, with nearly half its shaft, was drawn out and dropped into the ocean. Helplessly the two men-of-war rose and fell upon the waves.

In obedience to orders from the repeller, each crab took hold of one of the disabled vessels, and towed it near the mouth of the harbour, where it was left.

The city was now in a state of feverish excitement, which was intensified by the fact that a majority of the people did not understand what had happened, while those to whom this had been made plain could not comprehend why such a thing should have been allowed to happen. Three of Her Majesty's ships of war, equipped and ready for action, had sailed out of the harbour, and an apparently insignificant enemy, without firing a gun, had put them into such a condition that they were utterly unfit for service, and must be towed into a dry dock. How could the Government, the municipality, the army, or the navy explain this?

The anxiety, the excitement, the nervous desire to know what had happened, and what might be expected next, spread that evening to every part of the Dominion reached by telegraph.

The military authorities in charge of the defences of the city were as much disturbed and amazed by what had happened as any civilian could possibly be, but they had no fears for the safety of the place, for the enemy's vessels could not possibly enter, nor even approach, the harbour. The fortifications on the heights mounted guns much heavier than those on the men-of-war, and shots from these fired from an elevation might sink even those "underwater devils." But, more than on the forts, they relied upon their admirable system of torpedoes and submarine batteries. With these in position and ready for action, as they now were, it was impossible for an enemy's vessel, floating on the water or

Frank R. Stockton

under it, to enter the harbour without certain destruction.

Bulletins to this effect were posted in the city, and somewhat allayed the popular anxiety, although many people, who were fearful of what might happen next, left by the evening trains for the interior. That night the news of this extraordinary affair was cabled to Europe, and thence back to the United States, and all over the world. In many quarters the account was disbelieved, and in no quarter was it thoroughly understood, for it must be borne in mind that the methods of operation employed by the crabs were not evident to those on board the disabled vessels. But everywhere there was the greatest desire to know what would be done next.

It was the general opinion that the two armoured vessels were merely tenders to the submerged machines which had done the mischief. Having fired no guns, nor taken any active part in the combat, there was every reason to believe that they were intended merely as bomb-proof store-ships for their formidable consorts. As these submerged vessels could not attack a town, nor reduce fortifications, but could exercise their power only against vessels afloat, it was plain enough to see that the object of the American Syndicate was to blockade the port. That they would be able to maintain the blockade when the full power of the British navy should be brought to bear upon them was generally doubted, though it was conceded in the most wrathful circles that, until the situation should be altered, it would be unwise to risk valuable war vessels in encounters with the diabolical sea-monsters now lying off the port.

In the New York office of the Syndicate there was great satisfaction. The news received was incorrect and imperfect, but it was evident that, so far, everything had gone well.

About nine o'clock the next morning, Repeller No. 1, with her consort half a mile astern, and preceded by the two crabs, one on either bow, approached to within two miles of the harbour mouth. The crabs, a quarter of a mile ahead of the repeller, moved slowly; for between them they bore an immense net, three or four hundred feet long, and thirty feet deep, composed of jointed steel rods. Along the upper edge of this net was a series of air-floats, which were so graduated that they were sunk by the weight of the net a few feet below the surface of the water, from which position they held the net suspended vertically.

This net, which was intended to protect the repeller against the approach of submarine torpedoes, which might be directed from the shore, was anchored at each end, two very small buoys indicating its position. The crabs then falling astern, Repeller No. 1 lay to, with the sunken net between her and the shore, and prepared to project the first instantaneous motor-bomb ever used in warfare.

The great gun in the bow of the vessel was loaded with one of the largest and most powerful motor-bombs, and the spot to be aimed at was selected. This was a point in the water just inside of the mouth of the harbour, and nearly a mile from the land on either side. The distance of this point from the vessel being calculated, the cannon was adjusted at the angle called for by the scale of distances and levels, and the instrument indicating rise, fall, and direction was then put in connection with it.

Now the Director-in-chief stepped forward to the button, by pressing which the power of the motor was developed. The chief of the scientific corps then showed him the exact point upon the scale which would be indicated when the gun was in its proper position, and the piece was then moved upon its bearings so as to approximate as nearly as possible this direction.

The bow of the vessel now rose upon the swell of the sea,

Frank R. Stockton

and the instant that the index upon the scale reached the desired point, the Director-in-chief touched the button.

There was no report, no smoke, no visible sign that the motor had left the cannon; but at that instant there appeared, to those who were on the lookout, from a fort about a mile away, a vast aperture in the waters of the bay, which was variously described as from one hundred yards to five hundred yards in diameter. At that same instant, in the neighbouring headlands and islands far up the shores of the bay, and in every street and building of the city, there was felt a sharp shock, as if the underlying rocks had been struck by a gigantic trip-hammer.

At the same instant the sky above the spot where the motor had descended was darkened by a wide-spreading cloud. This was formed of that portion of the water of the bay which had been instantaneously raised to the height of about a thousand feet. The sudden appearance of this cloud was even more terrible than the yawning chasm in the waters of the bay or the startling shock; but it did not remain long in view. It had no sooner reached its highest elevation than it began to descend. There was a strong sea-breeze blowing, and in its descent this vast mass of water was impelled toward the land.

It came down, not as rain, but as the waters of a vast cataract, as though a mountain lake, by an earthquake shock, had been precipitated in a body upon a valley. Only one edge of it reached the land, and here the seething flood tore away earth, trees, and rocks, leaving behind it great chasms and gullies as it descended to the sea.

The bay itself, into which the vast body of the water fell, became a scene of surging madness. The towering walls of water which had stood up all around the suddenly created aperture hurled themselves back into the abyss, and down into the great chasm at the bottom of the bay, which had been made when the motor sent its shock along the great rock beds. Down upon, and into, this roaring, boiling tumult fell the tremendous cataract from above, and the harbour became one wild expanse of leaping maddened waves, hissing their whirling spray high into the air.

During these few terrific moments other things happened which passed unnoticed in the general consternation. All along the shores of the bay and in front of the city the waters seemed to be sucked away, slowly returning as the sea forced them to their level, and at many points up and down the harbour there were submarine detonations and upheavals of the water.

These were caused by the explosion, by concussion, of every torpedo and submarine battery in the harbour; and it was with this object in view that the instantaneous motor-bomb had been shot into the mouth of the bay.

The effects of the discharge of the motor-bomb astonished and even startled those on board the repellers and the crabs. At the instant of touching the button a hydraulic shock was felt on Repeller No. 1. This was supposed to be occasioned the discharge of the motor, but it was also felt on the other vessels. It was the same shock that had been felt on shore, but less in degree. A few moments after there was a great heaving swell of the sea, which tossed and rolled the four vessels, and lifted the steel protecting net so high that for an instant parts of it showed themselves above the surface like glistening sea-ghosts.

Experiments with motor-bombs had been made in unsettled mountainous districts, but this was the first one which had ever exerted its power under water.

On shore, in the forts, and in the city no one for an instant

Frank R. Stockton

supposed that the terrific phenomenon which had just occurred was in any way due to the vessels of the Syndicate. The repellers were in plain view, and it was evident that neither of them had fired a gun. Besides, the firing of cannon did not produce such effects. It was the general opinion that there had been an earthquake shock, accompanied by a cloud-burst and extraordinary convulsions of the sea. Such a combination of elementary disturbances had never been known in these parts; and a great many persons were much more frightened than if they had understood what had really happened.

In about half an hour after the discharge of the motor-bomb, when the sea had resumed its usual quiet, a boat carrying a white flag left Repeller No. 1, rowed directly over the submerged net, and made for the harbour. When the approach of this flag-of-truce was perceived from the fort nearest the mouth of the harbour, it occasioned much surmise. Had the earthquake brought these Syndicate knaves to their senses? Or were they about to make further absurd and outrageous demands? Some irate officers were of the opinion that enemies like these should be considered no better than pirates, and that their flag-of-truce should be fired upon. But the commandant of the fort paid no attention to such counsels, and sent a detachment with a white flag down to the beach to meet the approaching boat and learn its errand.

The men in the boat had nothing to do but to deliver a letter from the Director-in-chief to the commandant of the fort, and then row back again. No answer was required.

When the commandant read the brief note, he made no remark. In fact, he could think of no appropriate remark to make. The missive simply informed him that at ten o'clock and eighteen minutes A. M., of that day, the first bomb from the marine forces of the Syndicate had been discharged into the waters of the harbour. At, or about, two o'clock P.M., the second bomb would be discharged at Fort Pilcher. That was all.

What this extraordinary message meant could not be imagined by any officer of the garrison. If the people on board the ships were taking advantage of the earthquake, and supposed that they could induce British soldiers to believe that it had been caused by one of their bombs, then were they idiots indeed. They would fire their second shot at Fort Pilcher! This was impossible, for they had not yet fired their first shot. These Syndicate people were evidently very tricky, and the defenders of the port must therefore be very cautious.

Fort Pilcher was a very large and unfinished fortification, on a bluff on the opposite side of the harbour. Work had been discontinued on it as soon as the Syndicate's vessels had appeared off the port, for it was not desired to expose the builders and workmen to a possible bombardment. The place was now, therefore, almost deserted; but after the receipt of the Syndicate's message, the commandant feared that the enemy might throw an ordinary shell into the unfinished works, and he sent a boat across the bay to order away any workmen or others who might be lingering about the place.

A little after two o'clock P.M., an instantaneous motor-bomb was discharged from Repeller No. 1 into Fort Pilcher. It was set to act five seconds after impact with the object aimed at. It struck in a central portion of the unfinished fort, and having described a high curve in the air, descended not only with its own motive power, but with the force of gravitation, and penetrated deep into the earth.

Five seconds later a vast brown cloud appeared on the Fort Pilcher promontory. This cloud was nearly spherical in form, with an apparent diameter of about a thousand yards. At the same instant a shock similar to that accompanying the first motor-bomb was felt in the city and surrounding country; but this was not so severe as the other, for the second bomb did not exert its force upon the underlying rocks of the region as the first one had done.

The great brown cloud quickly began to lose its spherical form, part of it descending heavily to the earth, and part floating away in vast dust-clouds borne inland by the breeze, settling downward as they moved, and depositing on land, water, ships, houses, domes, and trees an almost impalpable powder.

When the cloud had cleared away there were no fortifications, and the bluff on which they had stood had disappeared. Part of this bluff had floated away on the wind, and part of it lay piled in great heaps of sand on the spot where its rocks were to have upheld a fort.

The effect of the motor-bomb was fully observed with glasses from the various fortifications of the port, and from many points of the city and harbour; and those familiar with the effects of explosives were not long in making up their minds what had happened. They felt sure that a mine had been sprung beneath Fort Pilcher; and they were now equally confident that in the morning a torpedo of novel and terrible power had been exploded in the harbour. They now disbelieved in the earthquake, and treated with contempt the pretence that shots had been fired from the Syndicate's vessel. This was merely a trick of the enemy. It was not even likely that the mine or the torpedo had been operated from the ship. These were, in all probability, under the control of confederates on shore, and had been exploded at times agreed upon beforehand. All this was perfectly plain to the military authorities.

But the people of the city derived no comfort from the announcement of these conclusions. For all that anybody knew the whole city might be undermined, and at any moment might ascend in a cloud of minute particles. They felt that they were in a region of hidden traitors and bombs, and in consequence of this belief thousands of citizens left their homes.

That afternoon a truce-boat again went out from Repeller No. 1, and rowed to the fort, where a letter to the commandant was delivered. This, like the other, demanded no answer, and the boat returned. Later in the afternoon the two repellers, accompanied by the crabs, and leaving the steel net still anchored in its place, retired a few miles seaward, where they prepared to lay to for the night.

The letter brought by the truce-boat was read by the commandant, surrounded by his officers. It stated that in twenty-four hours from time of writing it, which would be at or about four o'clock on the next afternoon, a bomb would be thrown into the garrisoned fort, under the command of the officer addressed. As this would result in the entire destruction of the fortification, the commandant was earnestly counselled to evacuate the fort before the hour specified.

Ordinarily the commandant of the fort was of a calm and unexcitable temperament. During the astounding events of that day and the day before he had kept his head cool; his judgment, if not correct, was the result of sober and earnest consideration. But now he lost his temper. The unparalleled effrontery and impertinence of this demand of the American Syndicate was too much for his self-possession. He stormed in anger.

Here was the culmination of the knavish trickery of these conscienceless pirates who had attacked the port. A torpedo had been exploded in the harbour, an unfinished fort had been mined and blown up, and all this had been done to frighten him—a British soldier—in command of a strong fort

Frank R. Stockton

well garrisoned and fully supplied with all the munitions of war. In the fear that his fort would be destroyed by a mystical bomb, he was expected to march to a place of safety with all his forces. If this should be done it would not be long before these crafty fellows would occupy the fort, and with its great guns turned inland, would hold the city at their mercy. There could be no greater insult to a soldier than to suppose that he could be gulled by a trick like this.

No thought of actual danger entered the mind of the commandant. It had been easy enough to sink a great torpedo in the harbour, and the unguarded bluffs of Fort Pilcher offered every opportunity to the scoundrels who may have worked at their mines through the nights of several months. But a mine under the fort which he commanded was an impossibility; its guarded outposts prevented any such method of attack. At a bomb, or a dozen, or a hundred of the Syndicate's bombs he snapped his fingers. He could throw bombs as well.

Nothing would please him better than that those ark-like ships in the offing should come near enough for an artillery fight. A few tons of solid shot and shell dropped on top of them might be a very conclusive answer to their impudent demands.

The letter from the Syndicate, together with his own convictions on the subject, were communicated by the commandant to the military authorities of the port, and to the War Office of the Dominion. The news of what had happened that day had already been cabled across the Atlantic back to the United States, and all over the world; and the profound impression created by it was intensified when it became known what the Syndicate proposed to do the next day. Orders and advices from the British Admiralty and War Office sped across the ocean, and that night few of the leaders in government circles in England or Canada closed their eyes.

The opinions of the commandant of the fort were received with but little favour by the military and naval authorities. Great preparations were already ordered to repel and crush this most audacious attack upon the port, but in the mean time it was highly desirable that the utmost caution and prudence should be observed. Three men-of-war had already been disabled by the novel and destructive machines of the enemy, and it had been ordered that for the present no more vessels of the British navy be allowed to approach the crabs of the Syndicate.

Whether it was a mine or a bomb which had been used in the destruction of the unfinished works of Fort Pilcher, it would be impossible to determine until an official survey had been made of the ruins; but, in any event, it would be wise and humane not to expose the garrison of the fort on the south side of the harbour to the danger which had overtaken the works on the opposite shore. If, contrary to the opinion of the commandant, the garrisoned fort were really mined, the following day would probably prove the fact. Until this point should be determined it would be highly judicious to temporarily evacuate the fort. This could not be followed by occupation of the works by the enemy, for all approaches, either by troops in boats or by bodies of confederates by land, could be fully covered by the inland redoubts and fortifications.

When the orders for evacuation reached the commandant of the fort, he protested hotly, and urged that his protest be considered. It was not until the command had been reiterated both from London and Ottawa, that he accepted the situation, and with bowed head prepared to leave his post. All night preparations for evacuation went on, and during the next morning the garrison left the fort, and established itself far enough away to preclude danger from the explosion of a

Frank R. Stockton

mine, but near enough to be available in case of necessity.

During this morning there arrived in the offing another Syndicate vessel. This had started from a northern part of the United States, before the repellers and the crabs, and it had been engaged in laying a private submarine cable, which should put the office of the Syndicate in New York in direct communication with its naval forces engaged with the enemy. Telegraphic connection between the cable boat and Repeller No. 1 having been established, the Syndicate soon received from its Director-in-chief full and comprehensive accounts of what had been done and what it was proposed to do. Great was the satisfaction among the members of the Syndicate when these direct and official reports came in. Up to this time they had been obliged to depend upon very unsatisfactory intelligence communicated from Europe, which had been supplemented by wild statements and rumours smuggled across the Canadian border.

To counteract the effect of these, a full report was immediately made by the Syndicate to the Government of the United States, and a bulletin distinctly describing what had happened was issued to the people of the country. These reports, which received a world-wide circulation in the newspapers, created a popular elation in the United States, and gave rise to serious apprehensions and concern in many other countries. But under both elation and concern there was a certain doubtfulness. So far the Syndicate had been successful; but its style of warfare was decidedly experimental, and its forces, in numerical strength at least, were weak. What would happen when the great naval power of Great Britain should be brought to bear upon the Syndicate, was a question whose probable answer was likely to cause apprehension and concern in the United States, and elation in many other countries.

The commencement of active hostilities had been

precipitated by this Syndicate. In England preparations were making by day an by night to send upon the coast-lines of the United States a fleet which, in numbers and power, would be greater than that of any naval expedition in the history of the world. It is no wonder that many people of sober judgment in America looked upon the affair of the crabs and the repellers as but an incident in the beginning of a great and disastrous war.

On the morning of the destruction of Fort Pilcher, the Syndicate's vessels moved toward the port, and the steel net was taken up by the two crabs, and moved nearer the mouth of the harbour, at a point from which the fort, now in process of evacuation, was in full view. When this had been done, Repeller No. 2 took up her position at a moderate distance behind the net, and the other vessels stationed themselves near by.

The protection of the net was considered necessary, for although there could be no reasonable doubt that all the torpedoes in the harbour and river had been exploded, others might be sent out against the Syndicate's vessels; and a torpedo under a crab or a repeller was the enemy most feared by the Syndicate.

About three o'clock the signals between the repellers became very frequent, and soon afterwards a truce-boat went out from Repeller No. 1. This was rowed with great rapidity, but it was obliged to go much farther up the harbour than on previous occasions, in order to deliver its message to an officer of the garrison.

This was to the effect that the evacuation of the fort had been observed from the Syndicate's vessels, and although it had been apparently complete, one of the scientific corps, with a powerful glass, had discovered a man in one of the outer redoubts, whose presence there was probably unknown to the

Frank R. Stockton

officers of the garrison. It was, therefore, earnestly urged that this man be instantly removed; and in order that this might be done, the discharge of the motor-bomb would be postponed half an hour.

The officer received this message, and was disposed to look upon it as a new trick; but as no time was to be lost, he sent a corporal's guard to the fort, and there discovered an Irish sergeant by the name of Kilsey, who had sworn an oath that if every other man in the fort ran away like a lot of addle-pated sheep, he would not run with them; he would stand to his post to the last, and when the couple of ships outside had got through bombarding the stout walls of the fort, the world would see that there was at least one British soldier who was not afraid of a bomb, be it little or big. Therefore he had managed to elude observation, and to remain behind.

The sergeant was so hot-headed in his determination to stand by the fort, that it required violence to remove him; and it was not until twenty minutes past four that the Syndicate observers perceived that he had been taken to the hill behind which the garrison was encamped.

As it had been decided that Repeller No. 2 should discharge the next instantaneous motor-bomb, there was an anxious desire on the part of the operators on that vessel that in this, their first experience, they might do their duty as well as their comrades on board the other repeller had done theirs. The most accurate observations, the most careful calculations, were made and re-made, the point to be aimed at being about the centre of the fort.

The motor-bomb had been in the cannon for nearly an hour, and everything had long been ready, when at precisely thirty minutes past four o'clock the signal to discharge came from the Director-in-chief; and in four seconds afterwards the index on the scale indicated that the gun was in the proper position, and the button was touched.

The motor-bomb was set to act the instant it should touch any portion of the fort, and the effect was different from that of the other bombs. There was a quick, hard shock, but it was all in the air. Thou-sands of panes of glass in the city and in houses for miles around were cracked or broken, birds fell dead or stunned upon the ground, and people on elevations at considerable distances felt as if they had received a blow; but there was no trembling of the ground.

As to the fort, it had entirely disappeared, its particles having been instantaneously removed to a great distance in every direction, falling over such a vast expanse of land and water that their descent was unobservable.

In the place where the fortress had stood there was a wide tract of bare earth, which looked as if it had been scraped into a staring dead level of gravel and clay. The instant-aneous motor-bomb had been arranged to act almost horizontally.

Few persons, except those who from a distance had been watching the fort with glasses, understood what had happ-ened; but every one in the city and surrounding country was conscious that something had happened of a most startling kind, and that it was over in the same instant in which they had perceived it. Everywhere there was the noise of falling window-glass. There were those who asserted that for an instant they had heard in the distance a grinding crash; and there were others who were quite sure that they had noticed what might be called a flash of darkness, as if something had, with almost unappreciable quickness, passed between them and the sun.

When the officers of the garrison mounted the hill before them and surveyed the place where their fort had been, there

Frank R. Stockton

was not one of them who had sufficient command of himself to write a report of what had happened. They gazed at the bare, staring flatness of the shorn bluff, and they looked at each other. This was not war. It was something supernatural, awful! They were not frightened; they were oppressed and appalled. But the military discipline of their minds soon exerted its force, and a brief account of the terrific event was transmitted to the authorities, and Sergeant Kilsey was sentenced to a month in the guard-house.

No one approached the vicinity of the bluff where the fort had stood, for danger might not be over; but every possible point of observation within a safe distance was soon crowded with anxious and terrified observers. A feeling of awe was noticeable everywhere. If people could have had a tangible idea of what had occurred, it would have been different. If the sea had raged, if a vast body of water had been thrown into the air, if a dense cloud had been suddenly ejected from the surface of the earth, they might have formed some opinion about it. But the instantaneous disappearance of a great fortification with a little more appreciable accompaniment than the sudden tap, as of a little hammer, upon thousands of window-panes, was something which their intellects could not grasp. It was not to be expected that the ordinary mind could appreciate the difference between the action of an instantaneous motor when imbedded in rocks and earth, and its effect, when opposed by nothing but stone walls, upon or near the surface of the earth.

Early the next morning, the little fleet of the Syndicate prepared to carry out its further orders. The waters of the lower bay were now entirely deserted, craft of every description having taken refuge in the upper part of the harbour near and above the city. Therefore, as soon as it was light enough to make observations, Repeller No. 1 did not hesitate to discharge a motor-bomb into the harbour, a mile or more above where the first one had fallen. This was done in order to explode any torpedoes which might have been put into position since the discharge of the first bomb.

There were very few people in the city and suburbs who were at that hour out of doors where they could see the great cloud of water arise toward the sky, and behold it descend like a mighty cataract upon the harbour and adjacent shores; but the quick, sharp shock which ran under the town made people spring from their beds; and although nothing was then to be seen, nearly everybody felt sure that the Syndicate's forces had begun their day's work by exploding another mine.

A lighthouse, the occupants of which had been ordered to leave when the fort was evacuated, as they might be in danger in case of a bombardment, was so shaken by the explosion of this motor-bomb that it fell in ruins on the rocks upon which it had stood.

The two crabs now took the steel net from its moorings and carried it up the harbour. This was rather difficult on account of the islands, rocks, and sand-bars; but the leading crab had on board a pilot acquainted with those waters. With the net hanging between them, the two submerged vessels, one carefully following the other, reached a point about two miles below the city, where the net was anchored across the harbour. It did not reach from shore to shore, but in the course of the morning two other nets, designed for shallower waters, were brought from the repellers and anchored at each end of the main net, thus forming a line of complete protection against submarine torpedoes which might be sent down from the upper harbour.

Repeller No. 1 now steamed into the harbour, accompanied by Crab A, and anchored about a quarter of a mile seaward of the net. The other repeller, with her attendant crab, cruised about the mouth of the harbour, watching a smaller entrance

Frank R. Stockton

to the port as well as the larger one, and thus maintaining an effective blockade. This was not a difficult duty, for since the news of the extraordinary performances of the crabs had been spread abroad, no merchant vessel, large or small, cared to approach that port; and strict orders had been issued by the British Admiralty that no vessel of the navy should, until further instructed, engage in combat with the peculiar craft of the Syndicate. Until a plan of action had been determined upon, it was very desirable that English cruisers should not be exposed to useless injury and danger.

This being the state of affairs, a message was sent from the office of the Syndicate across the border to the Dominion Government, which stated that the seaport city which had been attacked by the forces of the Syndicate now lay under the guns of its vessels, and in case of any overt act of war by Great Britain or Canada alone, such as the entrance of an armed force from British territory into the United States, or a capture of or attack upon an American vessel, naval or commercial, by a British man-of-war, or an attack upon an American port by British vessels, the city would be bombarded and destroyed.

This message, which was, of course, instantly transmitted to London, placed the British Government in the apparent position of being held by the throat by the American War Syndicate. But if the British Government, or the people of England or Canada, recognized this position at all, it was merely as a temporary condition. In a short time the most powerful men-of-war of the Royal Navy, as well as a fleet of transports carrying troops, would reach the coasts of North America, and then the condition of affairs would rapidly be changed. It was absurd to suppose that a few medium-sized vessels, however heavily armoured, or a few new-fangled submarine machines, however destructive they might be, could withstand an armada of the largest and finest armoured vessels in the world. A ship or two might be disabled, although this was unlikely, now that the new method of attack was understood; but it would soon be the ports of the United States, on both the Pacific and Atlantic coasts, which would lie under the guns of an enemy.

But it was not in the power of their navy that the British Government and the people of England and Canada placed their greatest trust, but in the incapacity of their petty foe to support its ridiculous assumptions. The claim that the city lay under the guns of the American Syndicate was considered ridiculous, for few people believed that these vessels had any guns. Certainly, there had been no evidence that any shots had been fired from them. In the opinion of reasonable people the destruction of the forts and the explosions in the harbour had been caused by mines—mines of a new and terrifying power—which were the work of traitors and confederates. The destruction of the lighthouse had strengthened this belief, for its fall was similar to that which would have been occasioned by a great explosion under its foundation.

But however terrifying and appalling had been the results of the explosion of these mines, it was not thought probable that there were any more of them. The explosions had taken place at exposed points distant from the city, and the most careful investigation failed to discover any present signs of mining operations.

This theory of mines worked by confederates was received throughout the civilized world, and was universally condemned. Even in the United States the feeling was so strong against this apparent alliance between the Syndicate and British traitors, that there was reason to believe that a popular pressure would be brought to bear upon the Government sufficient to force it to break its contract with the Syndicate, and to carry on the war with the National army and navy. The crab was considered an admirable

Frank R. Stockton

addition to the strength of the navy, but a mine under a fort, laid and fired by perfidious confederates, was considered unworthy an enlightened people.

The members of the Syndicate now found themselves in an embarrassing and dangerous position—a position in which they were placed by the universal incredulity regarding the instantaneous motor; and unless they could make the world believe that they really used such a motor-bomb, the war could not be prosecuted on the plan projected.

It was easy enough to convince the enemy of the terrible destruction the Syndicate was able to effect; but to make that enemy and the world understand that this was done by bombs, which could be used in one place as well as another, was difficult indeed. They had attempted to prove this by announcing that at a certain time a bomb should be projected into a certain fort. Precisely at the specified time the fort had been destroyed, but nobody believed that a bomb had been fired.

Every opinion, official or popular, concerning what it had done and what might be expected of it, was promptly forwarded to the Syndicate by its agents, and it was thus enabled to see very plainly indeed that the effect it had desired to produce had not been produced. Unless the enemy could be made to understand that any fort or ships within ten miles of one of the Syndicate's cannon could be instantaneously dissipated in the shape of fine dust, this war could not be carried on upon the principles adopted, and therefore might as well pass out of the hands of the Syndicate.

Day by day and night by night the state of affairs was anxiously considered at the office of the Syndicate in New York. A new and important undertaking was determined upon, and on the success of this the hopes of the Syndicate now depended.

During the rapid and vigorous preparations which the Syndicate were now making for their new venture, several events of interest occurred.

Two of the largest Atlantic mail steamers, carrying infantry and artillery troops, and conveyed by two swift and powerful men-of-war, arrived off the coast of Canada, considerably to the north of the blockaded city. The departure and probable time of arrival of these vessels had been telegraphed to the Syndicate, through one of the continental cables, and a repeller with two crabs had been for some days waiting for them. The English vessels had taken a high northern course, hoping they might enter the Gulf of St. Lawrence without subjecting themselves to injury from the enemy's crabs, it not being considered probable that there were enough of these vessels to patrol the entire coast. But although the crabs were few in number, the Syndicate was able to place them where they would be of most use; and when the English vessels arrived off the northern entrance to the gulf, they found their enemies there.

However strong might be the incredulity of the enemy regarding the powers of a repeller to bombard a city, the Syndicate felt sure there would be no present invasion of the United States from Canada; but it wished to convince the British Government that troops and munitions of war could not be safely transported across the Atlantic. On the other hand, the Syndicate very much objected to undertaking the imprisonment and sustenance of a large body of soldiers. Orders were therefore given to the officer in charge of the repeller not to molest the two transports, but to remove the rudders and extract the screws of the two war-vessels, leaving them to be towed into port by the troop-ships.

This duty was performed by the crabs, while the British vessels, both rams, were preparing to make a united and vigorous onset on the repeller, and the two men-of-war were left hopelessly tossing on the waves. One of the transports, a very fast steamer, had already entered the straits, and could not be signalled; but the other one returned and took both the war-ships in tow, proceeding very slowly until, after entering the gulf, she was relieved by tugboats.

Another event of a somewhat different character was the occasion of much excited feeling and comment, particularly in the United States. The descent and attack by British vessels on an Atlantic port was a matter of popular expectation. The Syndicate had repellers and crabs at the most important points; but, in the minds of naval officers and a large portion of the people, little dependence for defence was to be placed upon these. As to the ability of the War Syndicate to prevent invasion or attack by means of its threats to bombard the blockaded Canadian port, very few believed in it. Even if the Syndicate could do any more damage in that quarter, which was improbable, what was to prevent the British navy from playing the same game, and entering an American seaport, threaten to bombard the place if the Syndicate did not immediately run all their queer vessels high and dry on some convenient beach?

A feeling of indignation against the Syndicate had existed in the navy from the time that the war contract had been made, and this feeling increased daily. That the officers and men of the United States navy should be penned up in harbours, ports, and sounds, while British ships and the hulking mine-springers and rudder-pinchers of the Syndicate were allowed to roam the ocean at will, was a very hard thing for brave sailors to bear. Sometimes the resentment against this state of affairs rose almost to revolt.

The great naval preparations of England were not yet complete, but single British men-of-war were now frequently seen off the Atlantic coast of the United States. No American vessels had been captured by these since the message of the

Syndicate to the Dominion of Canada and the British Government. But one good reason for this was the fact that it was very difficult now to find upon the Atlantic ocean a vessel sailing under the American flag. As far as possible these had taken refuge in their own ports or in those of neutral countries.

At the mouth of Delaware Bay, behind the great Breakwater, was now collected a number of coastwise sailing-vessels and steamers of various classes and sizes; and for the protection of these maritime refugees, two vessels of the United States navy were stationed at this point. These were the Lenox and Stockbridge, two of the finest cruisers in the service, and commanded by two of the most restless and bravest officers of the American navy.

The appearance, early on a summer morning, of a large British cruiser off the mouth of the harbour, filled those two commanders with uncontrollable belligerency. That in time of war a vessel of the enemy should be allowed, undisturbed, to sail up and down before an American harbour, while an American vessel filled with brave American sailors lay inside like a cowed dog, was a thought which goaded the soul of each of these commanders. There was a certain rivalry between the two ships; and, considering the insult offered by the flaunting red cross in the offing, and the humiliating restrictions imposed by the Naval Department, each commander thought only of his own ship, and not at all of the other.

It was almost at the same time that the commanders of the two ships separately came to the conclusion that the proper way to protect the fleet behind the Breakwater was for his vessel to boldly steam out to sea and attack the British cruiser. If this vessel carried a long-range gun, what was to hinder her from suddenly running in closer and sending a few shells into the midst of the defenceless merchantmen? In

Frank R. Stockton

fact, to go out and fight her was the only way to protect the lives and property in the harbour.

It was true that one of those beastly repellers was sneaking about off the cape, accompanied, probably, by an underwater tongs-boat. But as neither of these had done anything, or seemed likely to do anything, the British cruiser should be attacked without loss of time.

When the commander of the Lenox came to this decision, his ship was well abreast of Cape Henlopen, and he therefore proceeded directly out to sea. There was a little fear in his mind that the English cruiser, which was now bearing to the south-east, might sail off and get away from him. The Stockbridge was detained by the arrival of a despatch boat from the shore with a message from the Naval Department. But as this message related only to the measurements of a certain deck gun, her commander intended, as soon as an answer could be sent off, to sail out and give battle to the British vessel.

Every soul on board the Lenox was now filled with fiery ardour. The ship was already in good fighting trim, but every possible preparation was made for a contest which should show their country and the world what American sailors were made of.

The Lenox had not proceeded more than a mile out to sea, when she perceived Repeller No. 6 coming toward her from seaward, and in a direction which indicated that it intended to run across her course. The Lenox, however, went straight on, and in a short time the two vessels were quite near each other. Upon the deck of the repeller now appeared the director in charge, who, with a speaking-trumpet, hailed the Lenox and requested her to lay to, as he had something to communicate. The commander of the Lenox, through his trumpet, answered that he wanted no communications, and advised the other vessel to keep out of his way.

The Lenox now put on a greater head of steam, and as she was in any case a much faster vessel than the repeller, she rapidly increased the distance between herself and the Syndicate's vessel, so that in a few moments hailing was impossible. Quick signals now shot up in jets of black smoke from the repeller, and in a very short time afterward the speed of the Lenox slackened so much that the repeller was able to come up with her.

When the two vessels were abreast of each other, and at a safe hailing distance apart, another signal went up from the repeller, and then both vessels almost ceased to move through the water, although the engines of the Lenox were working at high speed, with her propeller-blades stirring up a whirlpool at her stern.

For a minute or two the officers of the Lenox could not comprehend what had happened. It was first supposed that by mistake the engines had been slackened, but almost at the same moment that it was found that this was not the case, the discovery was made that the crab accompanying the repeller had laid hold of the stern-post of the Lenox, and with all the strength of her powerful engines was holding her back.

Now burst forth in the Lenox a storm of frenzied rage, such as was never seen perhaps upon any vessel since vessels were first built. From the commander to the stokers every heart was filled with fury at the insult which was put upon them. The commander roared through his trumpet that if that infernal sea-beetle were not immediately loosed from his ship he would first sink her and then the repeller.

To these remarks the director of the Syndicate's vessels paid no attention, but proceeded to state as briefly and forcibly as possible that the Lenox had been detained in order that he

Frank R. Stockton

might have an opportunity of speaking with her commander, and of informing him that his action in coming out of the harbour for the purpose of attacking a British vessel was in direct violation of the contract between the United States and the Syndicate having charge of the war, and that such action could not be allowed.

The commander of the Lenox paid no more attention to these words than the Syndicate's director had given to those he had spoken, but immediately commenced a violent attack upon the crab. It was impossible to bring any of the large guns to bear upon her, for she was almost under the stern of the Lenox; but every means of offence which infuriated ingenuity could suggest was used against it. Machine guns were trained to fire almost perpendicularly, and shot after shot was poured upon that portion of its glistening back which appeared above the water.

But as these projectiles seemed to have no effect upon the solid back of Crab H, two great anvils were hoisted at the end of the spanker-boom, and dropped, one after the other, upon it. The shocks were tremendous, but the internal construction of the crabs provided, by means of upright beams, against injury from attacks of this kind, and the great masses of iron slid off into the sea without doing any damage.

Finding it impossible to make any impression upon the mailed monster at his stern, the commander of the Lenox hailed the director of the repeller, and swore to him through his trumpet that if he did not immediately order the Lenox to be set free, her heaviest guns should be brought to bear upon his floating counting-house, and that it should be sunk, if it took all day to do it.

It would have been a grim satisfaction to the commander of the Lenox to sink Repeller No. 6, for he knew the vessel when she had belonged to the United States navy. Before she had been bought by the Syndicate, and fitted out with spring armour, he had made two long cruises in her, and he bitterly hated her, from her keel up.

The director of the repeller agreed to release the Lenox the instant her commander would consent to return to port. No answer was made to this proposition, but a dynamite gun on the Lenox was brought to bear upon the Syndicate's vessel. Desiring to avoid any complications which might ensue from actions of this sort, the repeller steamed ahead, while the director signalled Crab H to move the stern of the Lenox to the windward, which, being quickly done, the gun of the latter bore upon the distant coast.

It was now very plain to the Syndicate director that his words could have no effect upon the commander of the Lenox, and he therefore signalled Crab H to tow the United States vessel into port. When the commander of the Lenox saw that his vessel was beginning to move backward, he gave instant orders to put on all steam. But this was found to be useless, for when the dynamite gun was about to be fired, the engines had been ordered stopped, and the moment that the propeller-blades ceased moving the nippers of the crab had been released from their hold upon the stern-post, and the propeller-blades of the Lenox were gently but firmly seized in a grasp which included the rudder. It was therefore impossible for the engines of the vessel to revolve the propeller, and, unresistingly, the Lenox was towed, stern foremost, to the Breakwater.

The news of this incident created the wildest indignation in the United States navy, and throughout the country the condemnation of what was considered the insulting action of the Syndicate was general. In foreign countries the affair was the subject of a good deal of comment, but it was also the occasion of much serious consideration, for it proved that one of the Syndicate's submerged vessels could, without firing a gun, and without fear of injury to itself, capture a man-of-war and tow it whither it pleased.

The authorities at Washington took instant action on the affair, and as it was quite evident that the contract between the United States and the Syndicate had been violated by the Lenox, the commander of that vessel was reprimanded by the Secretary of the Navy, and enjoined that there should be no repetitions of his offence. But as the commander of the Lenox knew that the Secretary of the Navy was as angry as he was at what had happened, he did not feel his reprimand to be in any way a disgrace.

It may be stated that the Stockbridge, which had steamed for the open sea as soon as the business which had detained her was completed, did not go outside the Cape. When her officers perceived with their glasses that the Lenox was returning to port stern foremost, they opined what had happened, and desiring that their ship should do all her sailing in the natural way, the Stockbridge was put about and steamed, bow foremost, to her anchorage behind the Breakwater, the commander thanking his stars that for once the Lenox had got ahead of him.

The members of the Syndicate were very anxious to remove the unfavorable impression regarding what was called in many quarters their attack upon a United States vessel, and a circular to the public was issued, in which they expressed their deep regret at being obliged to interfere with so many brave officers and men in a moment of patriotic enthusiasm, and explaining how absolutely necessary it was that the Lenox should be removed from a position where a conflict with English line-of-battle ships would be probable. There were many thinking persons who saw the weight of the Syndicate's statements, but the effect of the circular upon the popular mind was not great.

The Syndicate was now hard at work making preparations for the grand stroke which had been determined upon. In the whole country there was scarcely a man whose ability could be made available in their work, who was not engaged in their service; and everywhere, in foundries, workshops, and ship-yards, the construction of their engines of war was being carried on by day and by night. No contracts were made for the delivery of work at certain times; everything was done under the direct supervision of the Syndicate and its subordinates, and the work went on with a definiteness and rapidity hitherto unknown in naval construction.

In the midst of the Syndicate's labours there arrived off the coast of Canada the first result of Great Britain's preparations for her war with the American Syndicate, in the shape of the Adamant, the largest and finest ironclad which had ever crossed the Atlantic, and which had been sent to raise the blockade of the Canadian port by the Syndicate's vessels.

This great ship had been especially fitted out to engage in combat with repellers and crabs. As far as was possible the peculiar construction of the Syndicate's vessels had been carefully studied, and English specialists in the line of naval construction and ordnance had given most earnest consideration to methods of attack and defence most likely to succeed with these novel ships of war. The Adamant was the only vessel which it had been possible to send out in so short a time, and her cruise was somewhat of an experiment. If she should be successful in raising the blockade of the Canadian port, the British Admiralty would have but little difficulty in dealing with the American Syndicate.

The most important object was to provide a defence against the screw-extracting and rudder-breaking crabs; and to this end the Adamant had been fitted with what was termed a "stern-jacket." This was a great cage of heavy steel bars,

Frank R. Stockton

which was attached to the stern of the vessel in such a way that it could be raised high above the water, so as to offer no impediment while under way, and which, in time of action, could be let down so as to surround and protect the rudder and screw-propellers, of which the Adamant had two.

This was considered an adequate defence against the nippers of a Syndicate crab; but as a means of offence against these almost submerged vessels a novel contrivance had been adopted. From a great boom projecting over the stern, a large ship's cannon was suspended perpendicularly, muzzle downward. This gun could be swung around to the deck, hoisted into a horizontal position, loaded with a heavy charge, a wooden plug keeping the load in position when the gun hung perpendicularly.

If the crab should come under the stern, this cannon could be fired directly downward upon her back, and it was not believed that any vessel of the kind could stand many such tremendous shocks. It was not known exactly how ventilation was supplied to the submarine vessels of the Syndicate, nor how the occupants were enabled to make the necessary observations during action. When under way the crabs sailed somewhat elevated above the water, but when engaged with an enemy only a small portion of their covering armour could be seen.

It was surmised that under and between some of the scales of this armour there was some arrangement of thick glasses, through which the necessary observation could be made; and it was believed that, even if the heavy perpendicular shots did not crush in the roof of a crab, these glasses would be shattered by concussion. Although this might appear a matter of slight importance, it was thought among naval officers it would necessitate the withdrawal of a crab from action.

In consequence of the idea that the crabs were vulnerable

between their overlapping plates, some of the Adamant's boats were fitted out with Gatling and machine guns, by which a shower of balls might be sent under the scales, through the glasses, and into the body of the crab. In addition to their guns, these boats would be supplied with other means of attack upon the crab.

Of course it would be impossible to destroy these submerged enemies by means of dynamite or torpedoes; for with two vessels in close proximity, the explosion of a torpedo would be as dangerous to the hull of one as to the other. The British Admiralty would not allow even the Adamant to explode torpedoes or dynamite under her own stern.

With regard to a repeller, or spring-armoured vessel, the Adamant would rely upon her exceptionally powerful armament, and upon her great weight and speed. She was fitted with twin screws and engines of the highest power, and it was believed that she would be able to overhaul, ram, and crush the largest vessel armoured or unarmoured which the Syndicate would be able to bring against her. Some of her guns were of immense calibre, firing shot weighing nearly two thousand pounds, and requiring half a ton of powder for each charge. Besides these she carried an unusually large number of large cannon and two dynamite guns. She was so heavily plated and armoured as to be proof against any known artillery in the world.

She was a floating fortress, with men enough to make up the population of a town, and with stores, ammunition, and coal sufficient to last for a long term of active service. Such was the mighty English battle-ship which had come forward to raise the siege of the Canadian port.

The officers of the Syndicate were well aware of the character of the Adamant, her armament and her defences, and had been informed by cable of her time of sailing and probable

Frank R. Stockton

destination. They sent out Repeller No. 7, with Crabs J and K, to meet her off the Banks of Newfoundland.

This repeller was the largest and strongest vessel that the Syndicate had ready for service. In addition to the spring armour with which these vessels were supplied, this one was furnished with a second coat of armour outside the first, the elastic steel ribs of which ran longitudinally and at right angles to those of the inner set. Both coats were furnished with a great number of improved air-buffers, and the arrangement of spring armour extended five or six feet beyond the massive steel plates with which the vessel was originally armoured. She carried one motor-cannon of large size.

One of the crabs was of the ordinary pattern, but Crab K was furnished with a spring armour above the heavy plates of her roof. This had been placed upon her after the news had been received by the Syndicate that the Adamant would carry a perpendicular cannon over her stern, but there had not been time enough to fit out another crab in the same way.

When the director in charge of Repeller No. 7 first caught sight of the Adamant, and scanned through his glass the vast proportions of the mighty ship which was rapidly steaming towards the coast, he felt that a responsibility rested upon him heavier than any which had yet been borne by an officer of the Syndicate; but he did not hesitate in the duty which he had been sent to perform, and immediately ordered the two crabs to advance to meet the Adamant, and to proceed to action according to the instructions which they had previously received. His own ship was kept, in pursuance of orders, several miles distant from the British ship.

As soon as the repeller had been sighted from the Adamant, a strict lookout had been kept for the approach of crabs; and when the small exposed portions of the backs of two of these were perceived glistening in the sunlight, the speed of the great ship slackened. The ability of the Syndicate's submerged vessels to move suddenly and quickly in any direction had been clearly demonstrated, and although a great ironclad with a ram could run down and sink a crab without feeling the concussion, it was known that it would be perfectly easy for the smaller craft to keep out of the way of its bulky antagonist. Therefore the Adamant did not try to ram the crabs, nor to get away from them. Her commander intended, if possible, to run down one or both of them; but he did not propose to do this in the usual way.

As the crabs approached, the stern-jacket of the Adamant was let down, and the engines were slowed. This stern-jacket, when protecting the rudder and propellers, looked very much like the cowcatcher of a locomotive, and was capable of being put to a somewhat similar use. It was the intention of the captain of the Adamant, should the crabs attempt to attach themselves to his stern, to suddenly put on all steam, reverse his engines, and back upon them, the stern-jacket answering as a ram.

The commander of the Adamant had no doubt that in this way he could run into a crab, roll it over in the water, and when it was lying bottom upward, like a floating cask, he could move his ship to a distance, and make a target of it. So desirous was this brave and somewhat facetious captain to try his new plan upon a crab, that he forebore to fire upon the two vessels of that class which were approaching him. Some of his guns were so mounted that their muzzles could be greatly depressed, and aimed at an object in the water not far from the ship. But these were not discharged, and, indeed, the crabs, which were new ones of unusual swiftness, were alongside the Adamant in an incredibly short time, and out of the range of these guns.

Crab J was on the starboard side of the Adamant, Crab K

was on the port side, and, simultaneously, the two laid hold of her. But they were not directly astern of the great vessel. Each had its nippers fastened to one side of the stern-jacket, near the hinge-like bolts which held it to the vessel, and on which it was raised and lowered.

In a moment the Adamant began to steam backward; but the only effect of this motion, which soon became rapid, was to swing the crabs around against her sides, and carry them with her. As the vessels were thus moving the great pincers of the crabs were twisted with tremendous force, the stern-jacket on one side was broken from its bolt, and on the other the bolt itself was drawn out of the side of the vessel. The nippers then opened, and the stern-jacket fell from their grasp into the sea, snapping in its fall the chain by which it had been raised and lowered.

This disaster occurred so quickly that few persons on board the Adamant knew what had happened. But the captain, who had seen everything, gave instant orders to go ahead at full speed. The first thing to be done was to get at a distance from those crabs, keep well away from them, and pound them to pieces with his heavy guns.

But the iron screw-propellers had scarcely begun to move in the opposite direction, before the two crabs, each now lying at right angles with the length of the ship, but neither of them directly astern of her, made a dash with open nippers, and Crab J fastened upon one propeller, while Crab K laid hold of the other. There was a din and crash of breaking metal, two shocks which were felt throughout the vessel, and the shattered and crushed blades of the propellers of the great battle-ship were powerless to move her.

The captain of the Adamant, pallid with fury, stood upon the poop. In a moment the crabs would be at his rudder! The great gun, double-shotted and ready to fire, was hanging from its boom over the stern. Crab K, whose roof had the additional protection of spring armour, now moved round so as to be directly astern of the Adamant. Before she could reach the rudder, her forward part came under the suspended cannon, and two massive steel shot were driven down upon her with a force sufficient to send them through masses of solid rock; but from the surface of elastic steel springs and air-buffers they bounced upward, one of them almost falling on the deck of the Adamant.

The gunners of this piece had been well trained. In a moment the boom was swung around, the cannon reloaded, and when Crab K fixed her nippers on the rudder of the Adamant, two more shot came down upon her. As in the first instance she dipped and rolled, but the ribs of her uninjured armour had scarcely sprung back into their places, before her nippers turned, and the rudder of the Adamant was broken in two, and the upper portion dragged from its fastenings then a quick backward jerk snapped its chains, and it was dropped into the sea.

A signal was now sent from Crab J to Repeller No. 7, to the effect that the Adamant had been rendered incapable of steaming or sailing, and that she lay subject to order.

Subject to order or not, the Adamant did not lie passive. Every gun on board which could be sufficiently depressed, was made ready to fire upon the crabs should they attempt to get away. Four large boats, furnished with machine guns, grapnels, and with various appliances which might be brought into use on a steel-plated roof, were lowered from their davits, and immediately began firing upon the exposed portions of the crabs. Their machine guns were loaded with small shells, and if these penetrated under the horizontal plates of a crab, and through the heavy glass which was supposed to be in these interstices, the crew of the submerged craft would be soon destroyed.

Frank R. Stockton

The quick eye of the captain of the Adamant had observed through his glass, while the crabs were still at a considerable distance, their protruding air-pipes, and he had instructed the officers in charge of the boats to make an especial attack upon these. If the air-pipes of a crab could be rendered useless, the crew must inevitably be smothered.

But the brave captain did not know that the condensed-air chambers of the crabs would supply their inmates for an hour or more without recourse to the outer air, and that the air-pipes, furnished with valves at the top, were always withdrawn under water during action with an enemy. Nor did he know that the glass blocks under the armour-plates of the crabs, which were placed in rubber frames to protect them from concussion above, were also guarded by steel netting from injury by small balls.

Valiantly the boats beset the crabs, keeping up a constant fusillade, and endeavouring to throw grapnels over them. If one of these should catch under an overlapping armour-plate it could be connected with the steam windlass of the Adamant, and a plate might be ripped off or a crab overturned.

But the crabs proved to be much more lively fish than their enemies had supposed. Turning, as if on a pivot, and darting from side to side, they seemed to be playing with the boats, and not trying to get away from them. The spring armour of Crab K interfered somewhat with its movements, and also put it in danger from attacks by grapnels, and it therefore left most of the work to its consort.

Crab J, after darting swiftly in and out among her antagonists for some time, suddenly made a turn, and dashing at one of the boats, ran under it, and raising it on its glistening back, rolled it, bottom upward, into the sea. In a moment the crew of the boat were swimming for their lives. They were quickly picked up by two of the other boats, which then deemed it prudent to return to the ship.

But the second officer of the Adamant, who commanded the fourth boat, did not give up the fight. Having noted the spring armour of Crab K, he believed that if he could get a grapnel between its steel ribs he yet might capture the sea-monster. For some minutes Crab K contented itself with eluding him; but, tired of this, it turned, and raising its huge nippers almost out of the water, it seized the bow of the boat, and gave it a gentle crunch, after which it released its hold and retired. The boat, leaking rapidly through two ragged holes, was rowed back to the ship, which it reached half full of water.

The great battle-ship, totally bereft of the power of moving herself, was now rolling in the trough of the sea, and a signal came from the repeller for Crab K to make fast to her and put her head to the wind. This was quickly done, the crab attaching itself to the stern-post of the Adamant by a pair of towing nippers. These were projected from the stern of the crab, and were so constructed that the larger vessel did not communicate all its motion to the smaller one, and could not run down upon it.

As soon as the Adamant was brought up with her head to the wind she opened fire upon the repeller. The latter vessel could easily have sailed out of the range of a motionless enemy, but her orders forbade this. Her director had been instructed by the Syndicate to expose his vessel to the fire of the Adamant's heavy guns. Accordingly the repeller steamed nearer, and turned her broadside toward the British ship.

Scarcely had this been done when the two great bow guns of the Adamant shook the air with tremendous roars, each hurling over the sea nearly a ton of steel. One of these great shot passed over the repeller, but the other struck her armoured side fairly amidship. There was a crash and scream of creaking steel, and Repeller No. 7 rolled over to windward as if she had been struck by a heavy sea. In a moment she righted and shot ahead, and, turning, presented her port side to the enemy. Instant examination of the armour on her other side showed that the two banks of springs were uninjured, and that not an air-buffer had exploded or failed to spring back to its normal length.

Firing from the Adamant now came thick and fast, the crab, in obedience to signals, turning her about so as to admit the firing of some heavy guns mounted amidships. Three enormous solid shot struck the repeller at different points on her starboard armour without inflicting damage, while the explosion of several shells which hit her had no more effect upon her elastic armour than the impact of the solid shot.

It was the desire of the Syndicate not only to demonstrate to its own satisfaction the efficiency of its spring armour, but to convince Great Britain that her heaviest guns on her mightiest battle-ships could have no effect upon its armoured vessels. To prove the absolute superiority of their means of offence and defence was the supreme object of the Syndicate. For this its members studied and worked by day and by night; for this they poured out their millions; for this they waged war. To prove what they claimed would be victory.

When Repeller No. 7 had sustained the heavy fire of the Adamant for about half an hour, it was considered that the strength of her armour had been sufficiently demonstrated; and, with a much lighter heart than when he had turned her broadside to the Adamant, her director gave orders that she should steam out of the range of the guns of the British ship. During the cannonade Crab J had quietly slipped away from the vicinity of the Adamant, and now joined the repeller.

The great ironclad battle-ship, with her lofty sides plated

with nearly two feet of solid steel, with her six great guns, each weighing more than a hundred tons, with her armament of other guns, machine cannon, and almost every appliance of naval warfare, with a small army of officers and men on board, was left in charge of Crab K, of which only a few square yards of armoured roof could be seen above the water. This little vessel now proceeded to tow southward her vast prize, uninjured, except that her rudder and propeller-blades were broken and useless.

Although the engines of the crab were of enormous power, the progress made was slow, for the Adamant was being towed stern foremost. It would have been easier to tow the great vessel had the crab been attached to her bow, but a ram which extended many feet under water rendered it dangerous for a submerged vessel to attach itself in its vicinity.

During the night the repeller kept company, although at a considerable distance, with the captured vessel; and early the next morning her director prepared to send to the Adamant a boat with a flag-of-truce, and a letter demanding the surrender and subsequent evacuation of the British ship. It was supposed that now, when the officers of the Adamant had had time to appreciate the fact that they had no control over the movements of their vessel; that their armament was powerless against their enemies; that the Adamant could be towed wherever the Syndicate chose to order, or left helpless in midocean,—they would be obliged to admit that there was nothing for them to do but to surrender.

But events proved that no such ideas had entered the minds of the Adamant's officers, and their action totally prevented sending a flag-of-truce boat. As soon as it was light enough to see the repeller the Adamant began firing great guns at her. She was too far away for the shot to strike her, but to launch and send a boat of any kind into a storm of shot and shell was of course impossible.

Frank R. Stockton

The cannon suspended over the stern of the Adamant was also again brought into play, and shot after shot was driven down upon the towing crab. Every ball rebounded from the spring armour, but the officer in charge of the crab became convinced that after a time this constant pounding, almost in the same place, would injure his vessel, and he signalled the repeller to that effect.

The director of Repeller No. 7 had been considering the situation. There was only one gun on the Adamant which could be brought to bear upon Crab K, and it would be the part of wisdom to interfere with the persistent use of this gun. Accordingly the bow of the repeller was brought to bear upon the Adamant, and her motor gun was aimed at the boom from which the cannon was suspended.

The projectile with which the cannon was loaded was not an instantaneous motor-bomb. It was simply a heavy solid shot, driven by an instantaneous motor attachment, and was thus impelled by the same power and in the same manner as the motor-bombs. The instantaneous motor-power had not yet been used at so great a distance as that between the repeller and the Adamant, and the occasion was one of intense interest to the small body of scientific men having charge of the aiming and firing.

The calculations of the distance, of the necessary elevation and direction, and of the degree of motor-power required, were made with careful exactness, and when the proper instant arrived the button was touched, and the shot with which the cannon was charged was instantaneously removed to a point in the ocean about a mile beyond the Adamant, accompanied by a large portion of the heavy boom at which the gun had been aimed.

The cannon which had been suspended from the end of this boom fell into the sea, and would have crashed down upon the roof of Crab K, had not that vessel, in obedience to a signal from the repeller, loosened its hold upon the Adamant and retired a short distance astern. Material injury might not have resulted from the fall of this great mass of metal upon the crab, but it was considered prudent not to take useless risks.

The officers of the Adamant were greatly surprised and chagrined by the fall of their gun, with which they had expected ultimately to pound in the roof of the crab. No damage had been done to the vessel except the removal of a portion of the boom, with some of the chains and blocks attached, and no one on board the British ship imagined for a moment that this injury had been occasioned by the distant repeller. It was supposed that the constant firing of the cannon had cracked the boom, and that it had suddenly snapped.

Even if there had been on board the Adamant the means for rigging up another arrangement of the kind for perpendicular artillery practice, it would have required a long time to get it into working order, and the director of Repeller No. 7 hoped that now the British captain would see the uselessness of continued resistance.

But the British captain saw nothing of the kind, and shot after shot from his guns were hurled high into the air, in hopes that the great curves described would bring some of them down on the deck of the repeller. If this beastly store-ship, which could stand fire but never returned it, could be sunk, the Adamant's captain would be happy. With the exception of the loss of her motive power, his vessel was intact, and if the stupid crab would only continue to keep the Adamant's head to the sea until the noise of her cannonade should attract some other British vessel to the scene, the condition of affairs might be altered.

Frank R. Stockton

All that day the great guns of the Adamant continued to roar. The next morning, however, the firing was not resumed, and the officers of the repeller were greatly surprised to see approaching from the British ship a boat carrying a white flag. This was a very welcome sight, and the arrival of the boat was awaited with eager interest.

During the night a council had been held on board the Adamant. Her cannonading had had no effect, either in bringing assistance or in injuring the enemy; she was being towed steadily southward farther and farther from the probable neighbourhood of a British man-of-war; and it was agreed that it would be the part of wisdom to come to terms with the Syndicate's vessel.

Therefore the captain of the Adamant sent a letter to the repeller, in which he stated to the persons in charge of that ship, that although his vessel had been injured in a manner totally at variance with the rules of naval warfare, he would overlook this fact and would agree to cease firing upon the Syndicate's vessels, provided that the submerged craft which was now made fast to his vessel should attach itself to the Adamant's bow, and by means of a suitable cable which she would furnish, would tow her into British waters. If this were done he would guarantee that the towing craft should have six hours in which to get away.

When this letter was read on board the repeller it created considerable merriment, and an answer was sent back that no conditions but those of absolute surrender could be received from the British ship.

In three minutes after this answer had been received by the captain of the Adamant, two shells went whirring and shrieking through the air toward Repeller No. 7, and after that the cannonading from the bow, the stern, the starboard, and the port guns of the great battle-ship went on whenever there was a visible object on the ocean which looked in the least like an American coasting vessel or man-of-war.

For a week Crab K towed steadily to the south this blazing and thundering marine citadel; and then the crab signalled to the still accompanying repeller that it must be relieved. It had not been fitted out for so long a cruise, and supplies were getting low.

The Syndicate, which had been kept informed of all the details of this affair, had already perceived the necessity of relieving Crab K, and another crab, well provisioned and fitted out, was already on the way to take its place. This was Crab C, possessing powerful engines, but in point of roof armour the weakest of its class. It could be better spared than any other crab to tow the Adamant, and as the British ship had not, and probably could not, put out another suspended cannon, it was considered quite suitable for the service required.

But when Crab C came within half a mile of the Adamant it stopped. It was evident that on board the British ship a steady lookout had been maintained for the approach of fresh crabs, for several enormous shell and shot from heavy guns, which had been trained upward at a high angle, now fell into the sea a short distance from the crab.

Crab C would not have feared these heavy shot had they been fired from an ordinary elevation; and although no other vessel in the Syndicate's service would have hesitated to run the terrible gauntlet, this one, by reason of errors in construction, being less able than any other crab to resist the fall from a great height of ponderous shot and shell, thought it prudent not to venture into this rain of iron; and, moving rapidly beyond the line of danger, it attempted to approach the Adamant from another quarter. If it could get within the circle of falling shot it would be safe. But this it could not do. On all sides of the Adamant guns had been trained to drop shot and shells at a distance of half a mile from the ship.

Around and around the mighty ironclad steamed Crab C; but wherever she went her presence was betrayed to the fine glasses on board the Adamant by the bit of her shining back and the ripple about it; and ever between her and the ship came down that hail of iron in masses of a quarter ton, half ton, or nearly a whole ton. Crab C could not venture under these, and all day she accompanied the Adamant on her voyage south, dashing to this side and that, and looking for the chance that did not come, for all day the cannon of the battle-ship roared at her wherever she might be.

The inmates of Crab K were now very restive and uneasy, for they were on short rations, both of food and water. They would have been glad enough to cast loose from the Adamant, and leave the spiteful ship to roll to her heart's content, broadside to the sea. They did not fear to run their vessel, with its thick roofplates protected by spring armour, through the heaviest cannonade.

But signals from the repeller commanded them to stay by the Adamant as long as they could hold out, and they were obliged to content themselves with a hope that when night fell the other crab would be able to get in under the stern of the Adamant, and make the desired exchange.

But to the great discomfiture of the Syndicate's forces, darkness had scarcely come on before four enormous electric lights blazed high up on the single lofty mast of the Adamant, lighting up the ocean for a mile on every side of the ship. It was of no more use for Crab C to try to get in now than in broad daylight; and all night the great guns roared, and the little crab manoeuvred.

The next morning a heavy fog fell upon the sea, and the battle-ship and Crab C were completely shut out of sight of each other. Now the cannon of the Adamant were silent, for the only result of firing would be to indicate to the crab the location of the British ship. The smoke-signals of the towing crab could not be seen through the fog by her consorts, and she seemed to be incapable of making signals by sound. Therefore the commander of the Adamant thought it likely that until the fog rose the crab could not find his ship.

What that other crab intended to do could be, of course, on board the Adamant, only a surmise; but it was believed that she would bring with her a torpedo to be exploded under the British ship. That one crab should tow her away from possible aid until another should bring a torpedo to fasten to her stern-post seemed a reasonable explanation of the action of the Syndicate's vessels.

The officers of the Adamant little understood the resources and intentions of their opponents. Every vessel of the Syndicate carried a magnetic indicator, which was designed to prevent collisions with iron vessels. This little instrument was placed at night and during fogs at the bow of the vessel, and a delicate arm of steel, which ordinarily pointed upward at a considerable angle, fell into a horizontal position when any large body of iron approached within a quarter of a mile, and, so falling, rang a small bell. Its point then turned toward the mass of iron.

Soon after the fog came on, one of these indicators, properly protected from the attraction of the metal about it, was put into position on Crab C. Before very long it indicated the proximity of the Adamant; and, guided by its steel point, the Crab moved quietly to the ironclad, attached itself to its stern-post, and allowed the happy crew of Crab K to depart coastward.

When the fog rose the glasses of the Adamant showed the approach of no crab, but it was observed, in looking over the stern, that the beggarly devil-fish which had the ship in tow appeared to have made some change in its back.

In the afternoon of that day a truce boat was sent from the repeller to the Adamant. It was allowed to come alongside; but when the British captain found that the Syndicate merely renewed its demand for his surrender, he waxed fiercely angry, and sent the boat back with the word that no further message need be sent to him unless it should be one complying with the conditions he had offered.

The Syndicate now gave up the task of inducing the captain of the Adamant to surrender. Crab C was commanded to continue towing the great ship southward, and to keep her well away from the coast, in order to avoid danger to seaport towns and coasting vessels, while the repeller steamed away.

Week after week the Adamant moved southward, roaring away with her great guns whenever an American sail came within possible range, and surrounding herself with a circle of bursting bombs to let any crab know what it might expect if it attempted to come near. Blazing and thundering, stern foremost, but stoutly, she rode the waves, ready to show the world that she was an impregnable British battle-ship, from which no enemy could snatch the royal colours which floated high above her.

It was during the first week of the involuntary cruise of the Adamant that the Syndicate finished its preparations for what it hoped would be the decisive movement of its campaign. To do this a repeller and six crabs, all with extraordinary powers, had been fitted out with great care, and also with great rapidity, for the British Government was working night and day to get its fleet of ironclads in readiness for a descent upon the American coast. Many of the British vessels were already well prepared for ordinary naval warfare; but to resist crabs additional defences were necessary. It was known that the Adamant had been captured, and consequently the manufacture of stern-jackets had been abandoned; but it was believed that protection could be effectually given to rudders and propeller-blades by a new method which the Admiralty had adopted.

The repeller which was to take part in the Syndicate's proposed movement had been a vessel of the United States navy which for a long time had been out of commission, and undergoing a course of very slow and desultory repairs in a dockyard. She had always been considered the most unlucky craft in the service, and nearly every accident that could happen to a ship had happened to her. Years and years before, when she would set out upon a cruise, her officers and crew would receive the humorous sympathy of their friends, and wagers were frequently laid in regard to the different kinds of mishaps which might befall this unlucky vessel, which was then known as the Tallapoosa.

The Syndicate did not particularly desire this vessel, but there was no other that could readily be made available for its purposes, and accordingly the Tallapoosa was purchased from the Government and work immediately begun upon her. Her engines and hull were put into good condition, and outside of her was built another hull, composed of heavy steel armour-plates, and strongly braced by great transverse beams running through the ship.

Still outside of this was placed an improved system of spring armour, much stronger and more effective than any which had yet been constructed. This, with the armour-plate, added nearly fifteen feet to the width of the vessel above water. All her superstructures were removed from her deck, which was covered by a curved steel roof, and under a bomb-proof

Frank R. Stockton

canopy at the bow were placed two guns capable of carrying the largest-sized motor-bombs. The Tallapoosa, thus transformed, was called Repeller No. 11.

The immense addition to her weight would of course interfere very much with the speed of the new repeller, but this was considered of little importance, as she would depend on her own engines only in time of action. She was now believed to possess more perfect defences than any battleship in the world.

Early on a misty morning, Repeller No. 11, towed by four of the swiftest and most powerful crabs, and followed by two others, left a Northern port of the United States, bound for the coast of Great Britain. Her course was a very northerly one, for the reason that the Syndicate had planned work for her to do while on her way across the Atlantic.

The Syndicate had now determined, without unnecessarily losing an hour, to plainly demonstrate the power of the instantaneous motor-bomb. It had been intended to do this upon the Adamant, but as it had been found impossible to induce the captain of that vessel to evacuate his ship, the Syndicate had declined to exhibit the efficiency of their new agent of destruction upon a disabled craft crowded with human beings.

This course had been highly prejudicial to the claims of the Syndicate, for as Repeller No. 7 had made no use in the contest with the Adamant of the motor-bombs with which she was said to be supplied, it was generally believed on both sides of the Atlantic that she carried no such bombs, and the conviction that the destruction at the Canadian port had been effected by means of mines continued as strong as it had ever been. To correct these false ideas was, now the duty of Repeller No. 11.

For some time Great Britain had been steadily forwarding troops and munitions of war to Canada, without interruption from her enemy. Only once had the Syndicate's vessels appeared above the Banks of Newfoundland, and as the number of these peculiar craft must necessarily be small, it was not supposed that their line of operations would be extended very far north, and no danger from them was apprehended, provided the English vessels laid their courses well to the north.

Shortly before the sailing of Repeller No. 11, the Syndicate had received news that one of the largest transatlantic mail steamers, loaded with troops and with heavy cannon for Canadian fortifications, and accompanied by the Craglevin, one of the largest ironclads in the Royal Navy, had started across the Atlantic. The first business of the repeller and her attendant crabs concerned these two vessels.

Owing to the power and speed of the crabs which towed her, Repeller No. 11 made excellent time; and on the morning of the third day out the two British vessels were sighted. Somewhat altering their course the Syndicate's vessels were soon within a few miles of the enemy.

The Craglevin was a magnificent warship. She was not quite so large as the Adamant, and she was unprovided with a stern-jacket or other defence of the kind. In sending her out the Admiralty had designed her to defend the transport against the regular vessels of the United States navy; for although the nature of the contract with the Syndicate was well understood in England, it was not supposed that the American Government would long consent to allow their war vessels to remain entirely idle.

When the captain of the Craglevin perceived the approach of the repeller he was much surprised, but he did not hesitate for a moment as to his course. He signalled to the transport,

Frank R. Stockton

then about a mile to the north, to keep on her way while he steered to meet the enemy. It had been decided in British naval circles that the proper thing to do in regard to a repeller was to ram her as quickly as possible. These vessels were necessarily slow and unwieldy, and if a heavy ironclad could keep clear of crabs long enough to rush down upon one, there was every reason to believe that the "ball-bouncer," as the repellers were called by British sailors, could be crushed in below the water-line and sunk. So, full of courage and determination, the captain of the Craglevin bore down upon the repeller.

It is not necessary to enter into details of the ensuing action. Before the Craglevin was within half a mile of her enemy she was seized by two crabs, all of which had cast loose from the repeller, and in less than twenty minutes both of her screws were extracted and her rudder shattered. In the mean time two of the swiftest crabs had pursued the transport, and, coming up with her, one of them had fastened to her rudder, without, however, making any attempt to injure it. When the captain of the steamer saw that one of the sea-devils had him by the stern, while another was near by ready to attack him, he prudently stopped his engines and lay to, the crab keeping his ship's head to the sea.

The captain of the Craglevin was a very different man from the captain of the Adamant. He was quite as brave, but he was wiser and more prudent. He saw that the transport had been captured and forced to lay to; he saw that the repeller mounted two heavy guns at her bow, and whatever might be the character of those guns, there could be no reasonable doubt that they were sufficient to sink an ordinary mail steamer. His own vessel was entirely out of his control, and even if he chose to try his guns on the spring armour of the repeller, it would probably result in the repeller turning her fire up on the transport.

With a disabled ship, and the lives of so many men in his charge, the captain of the Craglevin saw that it would be wrong for him to attempt to fight, and he did not fire a gun. With as much calmness as the circumstances would permit, he awaited the progress of events.

In a very short time a message came to him from Repeller No. 11, which stated that in two hours his ship would be destroyed by instantaneous motor-bombs. Every opportunity, however, would be given for the transfer to the mail steamer of all the officers and men on board the Craglevin, together with such of their possessions as they could take with them in that time. When this had been done the transport would be allowed to proceed on her way.

To this demand nothing but acquiescence was possible. Whether or not there was such a thing as an instantaneous motor-bomb the Craglevin's officers did not know; but they knew that if left to herself their ship would soon attend to her own sinking, for there was a terrible rent in her stern, owing to a pitch of the vessel while one of the propeller-shafts was being extracted.

Preparations for leaving the ship were, therefore, immediately begun. The crab was ordered to release the mail steamer, which, in obedience to signals from the Craglevin, steamed as near that vessel as safety would permit. Boats were lowered from both ships, and the work of transfer went on with great activity.

There was no lowering of flags on board the Craglevin, for the Syndicate attached no importance to such outward signs and formalities. If the captain of the British ship chose to haul down his colours he could do so; but if he preferred to leave them still bravely floating above his vessel he was equally welcome to do that.

Frank R. Stockton

When nearly every one had left the Craglevin, a boat was sent from the repeller, which lay near by, with a note requesting the captain and first officer of the British ship to come on board Repeller No. 11 and witness the method of discharging the instantaneous motor-bomb, after which they would be put on board the transport. This invitation struck the captain of the Craglevin with surprise, but a little reflection showed him that it would be wise to accept it. In the first place, it was in the nature of a command, which, in the presence of six crabs and a repeller, it would be ridiculous to disobey; and, moreover, he was moved by a desire to know something about the Syndicate's mysterious engine of destruction, if, indeed, such a thing really existed.

Accordingly, when all the others had left the ship, the captain of the Craglevin and his first officer came on board the repeller, curiously observing the spring armour over which they passed by means of alight gang-board with handrail. They were received by the director at one of the hatches of the steel deck, which were now all open, and conducted by him to the bomb-proof compartment in the bow. There was no reason why the nature of the repeller's defences should not be known to world nor adopted by other nations. They were intended as a protection against ordinary shot and shell; they would avail nothing against the instantaneous motor-bomb.

The British officers were shown the motor-bomb to be discharged, which, externally, was very much like an ordinary shell, except that it was nearly as long as the bore of the cannon; and the director stated that although, of course, the principle of the motor-bomb was the Syndicate's secret, it was highly desirable that its effects and its methods of operation should be generally known.

The repeller, accompanied by the mail steamer and all the crabs, now moved to about two miles to the leeward of the

Craglevin, and lay to. The motor-bomb was then placed in one of the great guns, while the scientific corps attended to the necessary calculations of distance, etc.

The director now turned to the British captain, who had been observing everything with the greatest interest, and, with a smile, asked him if he would like to commit hari-kari?

As this remark was somewhat enigmatical, the director went on to say that if it would be any gratification to the captain to destroy his vessel with his own hands, instead of allowing this to be done by an enemy, he was at liberty to do so. This offer was immediately accepted, for if his ship was really to be destroyed, the captain felt that he would like to do it himself.

When the calculations had been made and the indicator set, the captain was shown the button he must press, and stood waiting for the signal. He looked over the sea at the Craglevin, which had settled a little at the stern, and was rolling heavily; but she was still a magnificent battleship, with the red cross of England floating over her. He could not help the thought that if this motor mystery should amount to nothing, there was no reason why the Craglevin should not be towed into port, and be made again the grand warship that she had been.

Now the director gave the signal, and the captain, with his eyes fixed upon his ship, touched the button. A quick shock ran through the repeller, and a black-gray cloud, half a mile high, occupied the place of the British ship.

The cloud rapidly settled down, covering the water with a glittering scum which spread far and wide, and which had been the Craglevin.

The British captain stood for a moment motionless, and then

Frank R. Stockton

he picked up a rammer and ran it into the muzzle of the cannon which had been discharged. The great gun was empty. The instantaneous motor-bomb was not there.

Now he was convinced that the Syndicate had not mined the fortresses which they had destroyed.

In twenty minutes the two British officers were on board the transport, which then steamed rapidly westward. The crabs again took the repeller in tow, and the Syndicate's fleet continued its eastward course, passing through the wide expanse of glittering scum which had spread itself upon the sea.

They were not two-thirds of their way across the Atlantic when the transport reached St. John's, and the cable told the world that the Craglevin had been annihilated.

The news was received with amazement, and even consternation. It came from an officer in the Royal Navy, and how could it be doubted that a great man-of-war had been destroyed in a moment by one shot from the Syndicate's vessel! And yet, even now, there were persons who did doubt, and who asserted that the crabs might have placed a great torpedo under the Craglevin, that a wire attached to this torpedo ran out from the repeller, and that the British captain had merely fired the torpedo. But hour by hour, as fuller news came across the ocean, the number of these doubters became smaller and smaller.

In the midst of the great public excitement which now existed on both sides of the Atlantic,—in the midst of all the conflicting opinions, fears, and hopes,—the dominant sentiment seemed to be, in America as well as in Europe, one of curiosity. Were these six crabs and one repeller bound to the British Isles? And if so, what did they intend to do when they got there?

It was now generally admitted that one of the Syndicate's crabs could disable a man-of-war, that one of the Syndicate's repellers could withstand the heaviest artillery fire, and that one of the Syndicate's motor-bombs could destroy a vessel or a fort. But these things had been proved in isolated combats, where the new methods of attack and defence had had almost undisturbed opportunity for exhibiting their efficiency. But what could a repeller and half a dozen crabs do against the combined force of the Royal Navy,—a navy which had in the last few years regained its supremacy among the nations, and which had made Great Britain once more the first maritime power in the world?

The crabs might disable some men-of-war, the repeller might make her calculations and discharge her bomb at a ship or a fort, but what would the main body of the navy be doing meanwhile? Overwhelming, crushing, and sinking to the bottom crabs, repeller, motor guns, and everything that belonged to them.

In England there was a feeling of strong resentment that such a little fleet should be allowed to sail with such intent into British waters. This resentment extended itself, not only to the impudent Syndicate, but toward the Government; and the opposition party gained daily in strength. The opposition papers had been loud and reckless in their denunciations of the slowness and inadequacy of the naval preparations, and loaded the Government with the entire responsibility, not only of the damage which had already been done to the forts, the ships, and the prestige of Great Britain, but also for the threatened danger of a sudden descent of the Syndicate's fleet upon some unprotected point upon the coast. This fleet should never have been allowed to approach within a thousand miles of England. It should have been sunk in mid-ocean, if its sinking had involved the loss of a dozen men-of-war.

Frank R. Stockton

In America a very strong feeling of dissatisfaction showed itself. From the first, the Syndicate contract had not been popular; but the quick, effective, and business-like action of that body of men, and the marked success up to this time of their inventions and their operations, had caused a great reaction in their favour. They had, so far, successfully defended the American coast, and when they had increased the number of their vessels, they would have been relied upon to continue that defence. Even if a British armada had set out to cross the Atlantic, its movements must have been slow and cumbrous, and the swift and sudden strokes with which the Syndicate waged war could have been given by night and by day over thousands of miles of ocean.

Whether or not these strokes would have been quick enough or hard enough to turn back an armada might be a question; but there could be no question of the suicidal policy of sending seven ships and two cannon to conquer England. It seemed as if the success of the Syndicate had so puffed up its members with pride and confidence in their powers that they had come to believe that they had only to show themselves to conquer, whatever might be the conditions of the contest.

The destruction of the Syndicate's fleet would now be a heavy blow to the United States. It would produce an utter want of confidence in the councils and judgments of the Syndicate, which could not be counteracted by the strongest faith in the efficiency of their engines of war; and it was feared it might become necessary, even at this critical juncture, to annul the contract with the Syndicate, and to depend upon the American navy for the defence of the American coast.

Even among the men on board the Syndicate's fleet there were signs of doubt and apprehensions of evil. It had all been very well so far, but fighting one ship at a time was a very different thing from steaming into the midst of a hundred ships. On board the repeller there was now an additional reason for fears and misgivings. The unlucky character of the vessel when it had been the Tallapoosa was known, and not a few of the men imagined that it must now be time for some new disaster to this ill-starred craft, and if her evil genius had desired fresh disaster for her, it was certainly sending her into a good place to look for it.

But the Syndicate neither doubted nor hesitated nor paid any attention to the doubts and condemnations which they heard from every quarter. Four days after the news of the destruction of the Craglevin had been telegraphed from Canada to London, the Syndicate's fleet entered the English Channel. Owing to the power and speed of the crabs, Repeller No. 11 had made a passage of the Atlantic which in her old naval career would have been considered miraculous.

Craft of various kinds were now passed, but none of them carried the British flag. In the expectation of the arrival of the enemy, British merchantmen and fishing vessels had been advised to keep in the background until the British navy had concluded its business with the vessels of the American Syndicate.

As has been said before, the British Admiralty had adopted a new method of defence for the rudders and screw-propellers of naval vessels against the attacks of submerged craft. The work of constructing the new appliances had been pushed forward as fast as possible, but so far only one of these had been finished and attached to a man-of-war.

The Llangaron was a recently built ironclad of the same size and class as the Adamant; and to her had been attached the new stern-defence. This was an immense steel cylinder, entirely closed, and rounded at the ends. It was about ten feet in diameter, and strongly braced inside. It was suspended by chains from two davits which projected over the stern of the

Frank R. Stockton

vessel. When sailing this cylinder was hoisted up to the davits, but when the ship was prepared for action it was lowered until it lay, nearly submerged, abaft of the rudder. In this position its ends projected about fifteen feet on either side of the propeller-blades.

It was believed that this cylinder would effectually prevent a crab from getting near enough to the propeller or the rudder to do any damage. It could not be torn away as the stern-jacket had been, for the rounded and smooth sides and ends of the massive cylinder would offer no hold to the forceps of the crabs; and, approaching from any quarter, it would be impossible for these forceps to reach rudder or screw.

The Syndicate's little fleet arrived in British waters late in the day, and early the next morning it appeared about twenty miles to the south of the Isle of Wight, and headed to the north-east, as if it were making for Portsmouth. The course of these vessels greatly surprised the English Government and naval authorities. It was expected that an attack would probably be made upon some comparatively unprotected spot on the British seaboard, and therefore on the west coast of Ireland and in St. George's Channel preparations of the most formidable character had been made to defend British ports against Repeller No. 11 and her attendant crabs. Particularly was this the case in Bristol Channel, where a large number of ironclads were stationed, and which was to have been the destination of the Llangaron if the Syndicate's vessels had delayed their coming long enough to allow her to get around there. That this little fleet should have sailed straight for England's great naval stronghold was something that the British Admiralty could not understand. The fact was not appreciated that it was the object of the Syndicate to measure its strength with the greatest strength of the enemy. Anything less than this would not avail its purpose.

Notwithstanding that so many vessels had been sent to

different parts of the coast, there was still in Portsmouth harbour a large number of war vessels of various classes, all in commission and ready for action. The greater part of these had received orders to cruise that day in the channel. Consequently, it was still early in the morning when, around the eastern end of the Isle of Wight, there appeared a British fleet composed of fifteen of the finest ironclads, with several gunboats and cruisers, and a number of torpedo-boats.

It was a noble sight, for besides the warships there was another fleet hanging upon the outskirts of the first, and composed of craft, large and small, and from both sides of the channel, filled with those who were anxious to witness from afar the sea-fight which was to take place under such novel conditions. Many of these observers were reporters and special correspondents for great newspapers. On some of the vessels which came up from the French coast were men with marine glasses of extraordinary power, whose business it was to send an early and accurate report of the affair to the office of the War Syndicate in New York.

As soon as the British ships came in sight, the four crabs cast off from Repeller No. 11. Then with the other two they prepared for action, moving considerably in advance of the repeller, which now steamed forward very slowly. The wind was strong from the north-west, and the sea high, the shining tops of the crabs frequently disappearing under the waves.

The British fleet came steadily on, headed by the great Llangaron. This vessel was very much in advance of the others, for knowing that when she was really in action and the great cylinder which formed her stern-guard was lowered into the water her speed would be much retarded, she had put on all steam, and being the swiftest war-ship of her class, she had distanced all her consorts. It was highly important that she should begin the fight, and engage the attention of as many crabs as possible, while certain of the other ships

Frank R. Stockton

attacked the repeller with their rams. Although it was now generally believed that motor-bombs from a repeller might destroy a man-of-war, it was also considered probable that the accurate calculations which appeared to be necessary to precision of aim could not be made when the object of the aim was in rapid motion.

But whether or not one or more motor-bombs did strike the mark, or whether or not one or more vessels were blown into fine particles, there were a dozen ironclads in that fleet, each of whose commanders and officers were determined to run into that repeller and crush her, if so be they held together long enough to reach her.

The commanders of the torpedo-boats had orders to direct their swift messengers of destruction first against the crabs, for these vessels were far in advance of the repeller, and coming on with a rapidity which showed that they were determined upon mischief. If a torpedo, shot from a torpedo-boat, and speeding swiftly by its own powers beneath the waves, should strike the submerged hull of a crab, there would be one crab the less in the English Channel.

As has been said, the Llangaron came rushing on, distancing everything, even the torpedo-boats. If, before she was obliged to lower her cylinder, she could get near enough to the almost stationary repeller to take part in the attack on her, she would then be content to slacken speed and let the crabs nibble awhile at her stern.

Two of the latest constructed and largest crabs, Q and R, headed at full speed to meet the Llangaron, who, as she came on, opened the ball by sending a "rattler" in the shape of a five-hundred-pound shot into the ribs of the repeller, then at least four miles distant, and immediately after began firing her dynamite guns, which were of limited range at the roofs of the advancing crabs.

There were some on board the repeller who, at the moment the great shot struck her, with a ringing and clangour of steel springs, such as never was heard before, wished that in her former state of existence she had been some other vessel than the Tallapoosa.

But every spring sprang back to its place as the great mass of iron glanced off into the sea. The dynamite bombs flew over the tops of the crabs, whose rapid motions and slightly exposed surfaces gave little chance for accurate aim, and in a short time they were too close to the Llangaron for this class of gun to be used upon them.

As the crabs came nearer, the Llangaron lowered the great steel cylinder which hung across her stern, until it lay almost entirely under water, and abaft of her rudder and propeller-blades. She now moved slowly through the water, and her men greeted the advancing crabs with yells of defiance, and a shower of shot from machine guns.

The character of the new defence which had been fitted to the Llangaron was known to the Syndicate, and the directors of the two new crabs understood the heavy piece of work which lay before them. But their plans of action had been well considered, and they made straight for the stern of the British ship.

It was, of course, impossible to endeavour to grasp that great cylinder with its rounded ends; their forceps would slip from any portion of its smooth surface on which they should endeavour to lay hold, and no such attempt was made. Keeping near the cylinder, one at each end of it, the two moved slowly after the Llangaron, apparently discouraged.

In a short time, however, it was perceived by those on board the ship that a change had taken place in the appearance of the crabs; the visible portion of their backs was growing

Frank R. Stockton

larger and larger; they were rising in the water. Their mailed roofs became visible from end to end, and the crowd of observers looking down from the ship were amazed to see what large vessels they were.

Higher and higher the crabs arose, their powerful air-pumps working at their greatest capacity, until their ponderous pincers became visible above the water. Then into the minds of the officers of the Llangaron flashed the true object of this uprising, which to the crew had seemed an intention on the part of the sea-devils to clamber on board.

If the cylinder were left in its present position the crab might seize the chains by which it was suspended, while if it were raised it would cease to be a defence. Notwithstanding this latter contingency, the order was quickly given to raise the cylinder; but before the hoisting engine had been set in motion, Crab Q thrust forward her forceps over the top of the cylinder and held it down. Another thrust, and the iron jaws had grasped one of the two ponderous chains by which the cylinder was suspended. The other end of the cylinder began to rise, but at this moment Crab R, apparently by a single effort, lifted herself a foot higher out of the sea; her pincers flashed forward, and the other chain was grasped.

The two crabs were now placed in the most extraordinary position. The overhang of their roofs prevented an attack on their hulls by the Llangaron, but their unmailed hulls were so greatly exposed that a few shot from another ship could easily have destroyed them. But as any ship firing at them would be very likely to hit the Llangaron, their directors felt safe on this point.

Three of the foremost ironclads, less than two miles away, were heading directly for them, and their rams might be used with but little danger to the Llangaron; but, on the other hand, three swift crabs were heading directly for these ironclads.

It was impossible for Crabs Q and R to operate in the usual way. Their massive forceps, lying flat against the top of the cylinder, could not be twisted. The enormous chains they held could not be severed by the greatest pressure, and if both crabs backed at once they would probably do no more than tow the Llangaron stern foremost. There was, moreover, no time to waste in experiments, for other rams would be coming on, and there were not crabs enough to attend to them all.

No time was wasted. Q signalled to R, and R back again, and instantly the two crabs, each still grasping a chain of the cylinder, began to sink. On board the Llangaron an order was shouted to let out the cylinder chains; but as these chains had only been made long enough to allow the top of the cylinder to hang at or a little below the surface of the water, a foot or two of length was all that could be gained.

The davits from which the cylinder hung were thick and strong, and the iron windlasses to which the chains were attached were large and ponderous; but these were not strong enough to withstand the weight of two crabs with steel-armoured roofs, enormous engines, and iron hull. In less than a minute one davit snapped like a pipe-stem under the tremendous strain, and immediately afterward the windlass to which the chain was attached was torn from its bolts, and went crashing overboard, tearing away a portion of the stern-rail in its descent.

Crab Q instantly released the chain it had held, and in a moment the great cylinder hung almost perpendicularly from one chain. But only for a moment. The nippers of Crab R still firmly held the chain, and the tremendous leverage exerted by the falling of one end of the cylinder wrenched it from the rigidly held end of its chain, and, in a flash, the

Frank R. Stockton

enormous stern-guard of the Llangaron sunk, end foremost, to the bottom of the channel.

In ten minutes afterward, the Llangaron, rudderless, and with the blades of her propellers shivered and crushed, was slowly turning her starboard to the wind and the sea, and beginning to roll like a log of eight thousand tons.

Besides the Llangaron, three ironclads were now drifting broadside to the sea. But there was no time to succour disabled vessels, for the rest of the fleet was coming on, and there was great work for the crabs.

Against these enemies, swift of motion and sudden in action, the torpedo-boats found it almost impossible to operate, for the British ships and the crabs were so rapidly nearing each other that a torpedo sent out against an enemy was more than likely to run against the hull of a friend. Each crab sped at the top of its speed for a ship, not only to attack, but also to protect itself.

Once only did the crabs give the torpedo-boats a chance. A mile or two north of the scene of action, a large cruiser was making her way rapidly toward the repeller, which was still lying almost motionless, four miles to the westward. As it was highly probable that this vessel carried dynamite guns, Crab Q, which was the fastest of her class, was signalled to go after her. She had scarcely begun her course across the open space of sea before a torpedo-boat was in pursuit. Fast as was the latter, the crab was faster, and quite as easily managed. She was in a position of great danger, and her only safety lay in keeping herself on a line between the torpedo-boat and the gun-boat, and to shorten as quickly as possible the distance between herself and that vessel.

If the torpedo-boat shot to one side in order to get the crab out of line, the crab, its back sometimes hidden by the tossing waves, sped also to the same side. When the torpedo-boat could aim a gun at the crab and not at the gun-boat, a deadly torpedo flew into the sea; but a tossing sea and a shifting target were unfavourable to the gunner's aim. It was not long, however, before the crab had run the chase which might so readily have been fatal to it, and was so near the gun-boat that no more torpedoes could be fired at it.

Of course the officers and crew of the gun-boat had watched with most anxious interest the chase of the crab. The vessel was one which had been fitted out for service with dynamite guns, of which she carried some of very long range for this class of artillery, and she had been ordered to get astern of the repeller and to do her best to put a few dynamite bombs on board of her.

The dynamite gun-boat therefore had kept ahead at full speed, determined to carry out her instructions if she should be allowed to do so; but her speed was not as great as that of a crab, and when the torpedo-boat had given up the chase, and the dreaded crab was drawing swiftly near, the captain thought it time for bravery to give place to prudence. With the large amount of explosive material of the most tremendous and terrific character which he had on board, it would be the insanity of courage for him to allow his comparatively small vessel to be racked, shaken, and partially shivered by the powerful jaws of the on-coming foe. As he could neither fly nor fight, he hauled down his flag in token of surrender, the first instance of the kind which had occurred in this war.

When the director of Crab Q, through his lookout- glass, beheld this action on the part of the gun-boat, he was a little perplexed as to what he should next do. To accept the surrender of the British vessel, and to assume control of her, it was necessary to communicate with her. The communications of the crabs were made entirely by black-smoke signals, and these the captain of the gun-boat could not

Frank R. Stockton

understand. The heavy hatches in the mailed roof which could be put in use when the crab was cruising, could not be opened when she was at her fighting depth, and in a tossing sea.

A means was soon devised of communicating with the gun-boat. A speaking-tube was run up through one of the air-pipes of the crab, which pipe was then elevated some distance above the surface. Through this the director hailed the other vessel, and as the air-pipe was near the stern of the crab, and therefore at a distance from the only visible portion of the turtle-back roof, his voice seemed to come out of the depths of the ocean.

The surrender was accepted, and the captain of the gun-boat was ordered to stop his engines and prepare to be towed. When this order had been given, the crab moved round to the bow of the gun-boat, and grasping the cut-water with its forceps, reversed its engines and began to back rapidly toward the British fleet, taking with it the captured vessel as a protection against torpedoes while in transit.

The crab slowed up not far from one of the foremost of the British ships, and coming round to the quarter of the gun-boat, the astonished captain of that vessel was informed, through the speaking-tube, that if he would give his parole to keep out of this fight, he would be allowed to proceed to his anchorage in Portsmouth harbour. The parole was given, and the dynamite gun-boat, after reporting to the flag-ship, steamed away to Portsmouth.

The situation now became one which was unparalleled in the history of naval warfare. On the side of the British, seven war-ships were disabled and drifting slowly to the south-east. For half an hour no advance had been made by the British fleet, for whenever one of the large vessels had steamed ahead, such vessel had become the victim of a crab, and the

Vice-Admiral commanding the fleet had signalled not to advance until farther orders.

The crabs were also lying-to, each to the windward of, and not far from, one of the British ships. They had ceased to make any attacks, and were resting quietly under protection of the enemy. This, with the fact that the repeller still lay four miles away, without any apparent intention of taking part in the battle, gave the situation its peculiar character.

The British Vice-Admiral did not intend to remain in this quiescent condition. It was, of course, useless to order forth his ironclads, simply to see them disabled and set adrift. There was another arm of the service which evidently could be used with better effect upon this peculiar foe than could the great battle-ships.

But before doing anything else, he must provide for the safety of those of his vessels which had been rendered helpless by the crabs, and some of which were now drifting dangerously near to each other. Despatches had been sent to Portsmouth for tugs, but it would not do to wait until these arrived, and a sufficient number of ironclads were detailed to tow their injured consorts into port.

When this order had been given, the Vice-Admiral immediately prepared to renew the fight, and this time his efforts were to be directed entirely against the repeller. It would be useless to devote any further attention to the crabs, especially in their present positions. But if the chief vessel of the Syndicate's fleet, with its spring armour and its terrible earthquake bombs, could be destroyed, it was quite possible that those sea-parasites, the crabs, could also be disposed of.

Every torpedo-boat was now ordered to the front, and in a long line, almost abreast of each other, these swift vessels—the light-infantry of the sea—advanced upon the solitary and distant foe. If one torpedo could but reach her hull, the Vice-Admiral, in spite of seven disabled ironclads and a captured gun-boat, might yet gaze proudly at his floating flag, even if his own ship should be drifting broadside to the sea.

The line of torpedo-boats, slightly curving inward, had advanced about a mile, when Repeller No. 11 awoke from her seeming sleep, and began to act. The two great guns at her bow were trained upward, so that a bomb discharged from them would fall into the sea a mile and a half ahead. Slowly turning her bow from side to side, so that the guns would cover a range of nearly half a circle, the instantaneous motor-bombs of the repeller were discharged, one every half minute.

One of the most appalling characteristics of the motor-bombs was the silence which accompanied their discharge and action. No noise was heard, except the flash of sound occasioned by the removal of the particles of the object aimed at, and the subsequent roar of wind or fall of water.

As each motor-bomb dropped into the channel, a dense cloud appeared high in the air, above a roaring, seething cauldron, hollowed out of the waters and out of the very bottom of the channel. Into this chasm the cloud quickly came down, condensed into a vast body of water, which fell, with the roar of a cyclone, into the dreadful abyss from which it had been torn, before the hissing walls of the great hollow had half filled it with their sweeping surges. The piled-up mass of the redundant water was still sending its maddened billows tossing and writhing in every direction toward their normal level, when another bomb was discharged; another surging abyss appeared, another roar of wind and water was heard, and another mountain of furious billows uplifted itself in a storm of spray and foam, raging that it had found its place usurped.

Slowly turning, the repeller discharged bomb after bomb, building up out of the very sea itself a barrier against its enemies. Under these thundering cataracts, born in an instant, and coming down all at once in a plunging storm; into these abysses, with walls of water and floors of cleft and shivered rocks; through this wide belt of raging turmoil, thrown into new frenzy after the discharge of every bomb,— no vessel, no torpedo, could pass.

The air driven off in every direction by tremendous and successive concussions came rushing back in shrieking gales, which tore up the waves into blinding foam. For miles in every direction the sea swelled and upheaved into great peaked waves, the repeller rising upon these almost high enough to look down into the awful chasms which her bombs were making. A torpedo-boat caught in one of the returning gales was hurled forward almost on her beam ends until she was under the edge of one of the vast masses of descending water. The flood which, from even the outer limits of this falling-sea, poured upon and into the unlucky vessel nearly swamped her, and when she was swept back by the rushing waves into less stormy waters, her officers and crew leaped into their boats and deserted her. By rare good-fortune their boats were kept afloat in the turbulent sea until they reached the nearest torpedo-vessel.

Five minutes afterward a small but carefully aimed motor-bomb struck the nearly swamped vessel, and with the roar of all her own torpedoes she passed into nothing.

The British Vice-Admiral had carefully watched the repeller through his glass, and he noticed that simultaneously with the appearance of the cloud in the air produced by the action of the motor-bombs there were two puffs of black smoke from the repeller. These were signals to the crabs to notify them that a motor-gun had been discharged, and thus to provide against accidents in case a bomb should fail to act.

One puff signified that a bomb had been discharged to the north; two, that it had gone eastward; and so on. if, therefore, a crab should see a signal of this kind, and perceive no signs of the action of a bomb, it would be careful not to approach the repeller from the quarter indicated. It is true that in case of the failure of a bomb to act, another bomb would be dropped upon the same spot, but the instructions of the War Syndicate provided that every possible precaution should be taken against accidents.

Of course the Vice-Admiral did not understand these signals, nor did he know that they were signals, but he knew that they accompanied the discharge of a motor-gun. Once he noticed that there was a short cessation in the hitherto constant succession of water avalanches, and during this lull he had seen two puffs from the repeller, and the destruction, at the same moment, of the deserted torpedo-boat. It was, therefore, plain enough to him that if a motor-bomb could be placed so accurately upon one torpedo-boat, and with such terrible result, other bombs could quite as easily be discharged upon the other torpedo-boats which formed the advanced line of the fleet. When the barrier of storm and cataract again began to stretch itself in front of the repeller, he knew that not only was it impossible for the torpedo-boats to send their missives through this raging turmoil, but that each of these vessels was itself in danger of instantaneous destruction.

Unwilling, therefore, to expose his vessels to profitless danger, the Vice-Admiral ordered the torpedo-boats to retire from the front, and the whole line of them proceeded to a point north of the fleet, where they lay to.

When this had been done, the repeller ceased the discharge of bombs; but the sea was still heaving and tossing after the storm, when a despatch-boat brought orders from the British Admiralty to the flagship. Communication between the

British fleet and the shore, and consequently London, had been constant, and all that had occurred had been quickly made known to the Admiralty and the Government. The orders now received by the Vice-Admiral were to the effect that it was considered judicious to discontinue the conflict for the day, and that he and his whole fleet should return to Portsmouth to receive further orders.

In issuing these commands the British Government was actuated simply by motives of humanity and common sense. The British fleet was thoroughly prepared for ordinary naval warfare, but an enemy had inaugurated another kind of naval warfare, for which it was not prepared. It was, therefore, decided to withdraw the ships until they should be prepared for the new kind of warfare. To allow ironclad after ironclad to be disabled and set adrift, to subject every ship in the fleet to the danger of instantaneous destruction, and all this without the possibility of inflicting injury upon the enemy, would not be bravery; it would be stupidity. It was surely possible to devise a means for destroying the seven hostile ships now in British waters. Until action for this end could be taken, it was the part of wisdom for the British navy to confine itself to the protection of British ports.

When the fleet began to move toward the Isle of Wight, the six crabs, which had been lying quietly among and under the protection of their enemies, withdrew southward, and, making a slight circuit, joined the repeller.

Each of the disabled ironclads was now in tow of a sister vessel, or of tugs, except the Llangaron. This great ship had been disabled so early in the contest, and her broadside had presented such a vast surface to the north-west wind, that she had drifted much farther to the south than any other vessel. Consequently, before the arrival of the tugs which had been sent for to tow her into harbour, the Llangaron was well on her way across the channel. A foggy night came on, and the

Frank R. Stockton

next morning she was ashore on the coast of France, with a mile of water between her and dry land. Fast-rooted in a great sand-bank, she lay week after week, with the storms that came in from the Atlantic, and the storms that came in from the German Ocean, beating upon her tall side of solid iron, with no more effect than if it had been a precipice of rock. Against waves and winds she formed a massive breakwater, with a wide stretch of smooth sea between her and the land. There she lay, proof against all the artillery of Europe, and all the artillery of the sea and the storm, until a fleet of small vessels had taken from her her ponderous armament, her coal and stores, and she had been lightened enough to float upon a high tide, and to follow three tugs to Portsmouth.

When night came on, Repeller No. 11 and the crabs dropped down with the tide, and lay to some miles west of the scene of battle. The fog shut them in fairly well, but, fearful that torpedoes might be sent out against them, they showed no lights. There was little danger, of collision with passing merchantmen, for the English Channel, at present, was deserted by this class of vessels.

The next morning the repeller, preceded by two crabs, bearing between them a submerged net similar to that used at the Canadian port, appeared off the eastern end of the Isle of Wight. The anchors of the net were dropped, and behind it the repeller took her place, and shortly afterward she sent a flag-of-truce boat to Portsmouth harbour. This boat carried a note from the American War Syndicate to the British Government.

In this note it was stated that it was now the intention of the Syndicate to utterly destroy, by means of the instantaneous motor, a fortified post upon the British coast. As this would be done solely for the purpose of demonstrating the irresistible destructive power of the motor-bombs, it was immaterial to the Syndicate what fortified post should be destroyed, provided it should answer the requirements of the proposed demonstration. Consequently the British Government was offered the opportunity of naming the fortified place which should be destroyed. If said Government should decline to do this, or delay the selection for twenty-four hours, the Syndicate would itself decide upon the place to be operated upon.

Every one in every branch of the British Government, and, in fact, nearly every thinking person in the British islands, had been racking his brains, or her brains, that night, over the astounding situation; and the note of the Syndicate only added to the perturbation of the Government. There was a strong feeling in official circles that the insolent little enemy must be crushed, if the whole British navy should have to rush upon it, and all sink together in a common grave.

But there were cooler and more prudent brains at the head of affairs; and these had already decided that the contest between the old engines of war and the new ones was entirely one-sided. The instincts of good government dictated to them that they should be extremely wary and circumspect during the further continuance of this unexampled war. Therefore, when the note of the Syndicate was considered, it was agreed that the time had come when good statesmanship and wise diplomacy would be more valuable to the nation than torpedoes, armoured ships, or heavy guns.

There was not the slightest doubt that the country would disagree with the Government, but on the latter lay the responsibility of the country's safety. There was nothing, in the opinion of the ablest naval officers, to prevent the Syndicate's fleet from coming up the Thames. Instantaneous motor-bombs could sweep away all forts and citadels, and explode and destroy all torpedo defences, and London might lie under the guns of the repeller.

In consequence of this view of the state of affairs, an answer was sent to the Syndicate's note, asking that further time be given for the consideration of the situation, and suggesting that an exhibition of the power of the motor-bomb was not necessary, as sufficient proof of this had been given in the destruction of the Canadian forts, the annihilation of the Craglevin, and the extraordinary results of the discharge of said bombs on the preceding day.

To this a reply was sent from the office of the Syndicate in New York, by means of a cable boat from the French coast, that on no account could their purpose be altered or their propositions modified. Although the British Government might be convinced of the power of the Syndicate's motor-bombs, it was not the case with the British people, for it was yet popularly disbelieved that motor-bombs existed. This disbelief the Syndicate was determined to overcome, not only for the furtherance of its own purposes, but to prevent the downfall of the present British Ministry, and a probable radical change in the Government. That such a political revolution, as undesirable to the Syndicate as to cool-headed and sensible Englishmen, was imminent, there could be no doubt. The growing feeling of disaffection, almost amounting to disloyalty, not only in the opposition party, but among those who had hitherto been firm adherents of the Government, was mainly based upon the idea that the present British rulers had allowed themselves to be frightened by mines and torpedoes, artfully placed and exploded. Therefore the Syndicate intended to set right the public mind upon this subject. The note concluded by earnestly urging the designation, without loss of time, of a place of operations.

This answer was received in London in the evening, and all night it was the subject of earnest and anxious deliberation in the Government offices. It was at last decided, amid great opposition, that the Syndicate's alternative must be accepted, for it would be the height of folly to allow the repeller to bombard any port she should choose. When this conclusion had been reached, the work of selecting a place for the proposed demonstration of the American Syndicate occupied but little time. The task was not difficult. Nowhere in Great Britain was there a fortified spot of so little importance as Caerdaff, on the west coast of Wales.

Caerdaff consisted of a large fort on a promontory, and an immense castellated structure on the other side of a small bay, with a little fishing village at the head of said bay. The castellated structure was rather old, the fortress somewhat less so; and both had long been considered useless, as there was no probability that an enemy would land at this point on the coast.

Caerdaff was therefore selected as the spot to be operated upon. No one could for a moment imagine that the Syndicate had mined this place; and if it should be destroyed by motor-bombs, it would prove to the country that the Government had not been frightened by the tricks of a crafty enemy.

An hour after the receipt of the note in which it was stated that Caerdaff had been selected, the Syndicate's fleet started for that place. The crabs were elevated to cruising height, the repeller taken in tow, and by the afternoon of the next day the fleet was lying off Caerdaff. A note was sent on shore to the officer in command, stating that the bombardment would begin at ten o'clock in the morning of the next day but one, and requesting that information of the hour appointed be instantly transmitted to London. When this had been done, the fleet steamed six or seven miles off shore, where it lay to or cruised about for two nights and a day.

As soon as the Government had selected Caerdaff for bombardment, immediate measures were taken to remove

Frank R. Stockton

the small garrisons and the inhabitants of the fishing village from possible danger. When the Syndicate's note was received by the commandant of the fort, he was already in receipt of orders from the War Office to evacuate the fortifications, and to superintend the removal of the fishermen and their families to a point of safety farther up the coast.

Caerdaff was a place difficult of access by land, the nearest railroad stations being fifteen or twenty miles away; but on the day after the arrival of the Syndicate's fleet in the offing, thousands of people made their way to this part of the country, anxious to see—if perchance they might find an opportunity to safely see—what might happen at ten o'clock the next morning. Officers of the army and navy, Government officials, press correspondents, in great numbers, and curious and anxious observers of all classes, hastened to the Welsh coast.

The little towns where the visitors left the trains were crowded to overflowing, and every possible conveyance, by which the mountains lying back of Caerdaff could be reached, was eagerly secured, many persons, however, being obliged to depend upon their own legs. Soon after sunrise of the appointed day the forts, the village, and the surrounding lower country were entirely deserted, and every point of vantage on the mountains lying some miles back from the coast was occupied by excited spectators, nearly every one armed with a field-glass.

A few of the guns from the fortifications were transported to an overlooking height, in order that they might be brought into action in case the repeller, instead of bombarding, should send men in boats to take possession of the evacuated fortifications, or should attempt any mining operations. The gunners for this battery were stationed at a safe place to the rear, whence they could readily reach their guns if necessary.

The next day was one of supreme importance to the Syndicate. On this day it must make plain to the world, not only what the motor-bomb could do, but that the motor-bomb did what was done. Before leaving the English Channel the director of Repeller No. 11 had received telegraphic advices from both Europe and America, indicating the general drift of public opinion in regard to the recent sea-fight; and, besides these, many English and continental papers had been brought to him from the French coast.

From all these the director perceived that the cause of the Syndicate had in a certain way suffered from the manner in which the battle in the channel had been conducted. Every newspaper urged that if the repeller carried guns capable of throwing the bombs which the Syndicate professed to use, there was no reason why every ship in the British fleet should not have been destroyed. But as the repeller had not fired a single shot at the fleet, and as the battle had been fought entirely by the crabs, there was every reason to believe that if there were such things as motor-guns, their range was very short, not as great as that of the ordinary dynamite cannon. The great risk run by one of the crabs in order to disable a dynamite gun-boat seemed an additional proof of this.

It was urged that the explosions in the water might have been produced by torpedoes; that the torpedo-boat which had been destroyed was so near the repeller that an ordinary shell was sufficient to accomplish the damage that had been done.

To gainsay these assumptions was imperative on the Syndicate's forces. To firmly establish the prestige of the instantaneous motor was the object of the war. Crabs were of but temporary service. Any nation could build vessels like them, and there were many means of destroying them. The spring armour was a complete defence against ordinary artillery, but

Frank R. Stockton

it was not a defence against submarine torpedoes. The claims of the Syndicate could be firmly based on nothing but the powers of absolute annihilation possessed by the instantaneous motor-bomb.

About nine o'clock on the appointed morning, Repeller No. 11, much to the surprise of the spectators on the high grounds with field-glasses and telescopes, steamed away from Caerdaff. What this meant nobody knew, but the naval military observers immediately suspected that the Syndicate's vessel had concentrated attention upon Caerdaff in order to go over to Ireland to do some sort of mischief there. It was presumed that the crabs accompanied her, but as they were now at their fighting depth it was impossible to see them at so great a distance.

But it was soon perceived that Repeller No. 11 had no intention of running away, nor of going over to Ireland. From slowly cruising about four or five miles off shore, she had steamed westward until she had reached a point which, according to the calculations of her scientific corps, was nine marine miles from Caerdaff. There she lay to against a strong breeze from the east.

It was not yet ten o'clock when the officer in charge of the starboard gun remarked to the director that he suppose that it would not be necessary to give the smoke signals, as had been done in the channel, as now all the crabs were lying near them. The director reflected a moment, and then ordered that the signals should be given at every discharge of the gun, and that the columns of black smoke should be shot up to their greatest height.

At precisely ten o'clock, up rose from Repeller No. 11 two tall jets of black smoke. Up rose from the promontory of Caerdaff, a heavy gray cloud, like an immense balloon, and then the people on the hill-tops and highlands felt a sharp shock of the ground and rocks beneath them, and heard the sound of a terrible but momentary grinding crush.

As the cloud began to settle, it was borne out to sea by the wind, and then it was revealed that the fortifications of Caerdaff had disappeared.

In ten minutes there was another smoke signal, and a great cloud over the castellated structure on the other side of the bay. The cloud passed away, leaving a vacant space on the other side of the bay.

The second shock sent a panic through the crowd of spectators. The next earthquake bomb might strike among them. Down the eastern slopes ran hundreds of them, leaving only a few of the bravest civilians, the reporters of the press, and the naval and military men.

The next motor-bomb descended into the fishing village, the comminuted particles of which, being mostly of light material, floated far out to sea.

The detachment of artillerists who had been deputed to man the guns on the heights which commanded the bay had been ordered to fall back to the mountains as soon as it had been seen that it was not the intention of the repeller to send boats on shore. The most courageous of the spectators trembled a little when the fourth bomb was discharged, for it came farther inland, and struck the height on which the battery had been placed, removing all vestiges of the guns, caissons, and the ledge of rock on which they had stood.

The motor-bombs which the repeller was now discharging were of the largest size and greatest power, and a dozen more of them were discharged at intervals of a few minutes. The promontory on which the fortifications had stood was annihilated, and the waters of the bay swept over its foundations. Soon afterward the head of the bay seemed madly rushing out to sea, but quickly surged back to fill the chasm which yawned at the spot where the village had been.

The dense clouds were now upheaved at such short intervals that the scene of devastation was completely shut out from the observers on the hills; but every few minutes they felt a sickening shock, and heard a momentary and horrible crash and hiss which seemed to fill all the air. The instantaneous motor-bombs were tearing up the sea-board, and grinding it to atoms.

It was not yet noon when the bombardment ceased. No more puffs of black smoke came up from the distant repeller, and the vast spreading mass of clouds moved seaward, dropping down upon St. George's Channel in a rain of stone dust. Then the repeller steamed shoreward, and when she was within three or four miles of the coast she ran up a large white flag in token that her task was ended.

This sign that the bombardment had ceased was accepted in good faith; and as some of the military and naval men had carefully noted that each puff from the repeller was accompanied by a shock, it was considered certain that all the bombs which had been discharged had acted, and that, consequently, no further danger was to be apprehended from them. In spite of this announcement many of the spectators would not leave their position on the hills, but a hundred or more of curious and courageous men ventured down into the plain.

That part of the sea-coast where Caerdaff had been was a new country, about which men wandered slowly and cautiously with sudden exclamations, of amazement and awe. There were no longer promontories jutting out into the sea; there were no hillocks and rocky terraces rising inland. In a vast plain, shaven and shorn down to a common level of scarred and pallid rock, there lay an immense chasm two miles and a half long, half a mile wide, and so deep that shuddering men could stand and look down upon the rent and riven rocks upon which had rested that portion of the Welsh coast which had now blown out to sea.

An officer of the Royal Engineers stood on the seaward edge of this yawning abyss; then he walked over to the almost circular body of water which occupied the place where the fishing village had been, and into which the waters of the bay had flowed. When this officer returned to London he wrote a report to the effect that a ship canal, less than an eighth of a mile long, leading from the newly formed lake at the head of the bay, would make of this chasm, when filled by the sea, the finest and most thoroughly protected inland basin for ships of all sizes on the British coast. But before this report received due official consideration the idea had been suggested and elaborated in a dozen newspapers.

Accounts and reports of all kinds describing the destruction of Caerdaff, and of the place in which it had stood, filled the newspapers of the world. Photo-graphs and pictures of Caerdaff as it had been and as it then was were produced with marvellous rapidity, and the earthquake bomb of the American War Syndicate was the subject of excited conversation in every civilized country.

The British Ministry was now the calmest body of men in Europe. The great opposition storm had died away, the great war storm had ceased, and the wisest British statesmen saw the unmistakable path of national policy lying plain and open before them. There was no longer time for arguments and struggles with opponents or enemies, internal or external. There was even no longer time for the discussion of measures. It was the time for the adoption of a measure which indicated itself, and which did not need discussion.

Frank R. Stockton

On the afternoon of the day of the bombardment of Caerdaff, Repeller No. 11, accompanied by her crabs, steamed for the English Channel. Two days afterward there lay off the coast at Brighton, with a white flag floating high above her, the old Tallapoosa, now naval mistress of the world.

Near by lay a cable boat, and constant communication by way of France was kept up between the officers of the American Syndicate and the repeller. In a very short time communications were opened between the repeller and London.

When this last step became known to the public of America, almost as much excited by the recent events as the public of England, a great disturbance arose in certain political circles. It was argued that the Syndicate had no right to negotiate in any way with the Government of England; that it had been empowered to carry on a war; and that, if its duties in this regard had been satisfactorily executed, it must now retire, and allow the United States Government to attend to its foreign relations.

But the Syndicate was firm. It had contracted to bring the war to a satisfactory conclusion. When it considered that this had been done, it would retire and allow the American Government, with whom the contract had been made, to decide whether or not it had been properly performed.

The unmistakable path of national policy which had shown itself to the wisest British statesmen appeared broader and plainer when the overtures of the American War Syndicate had been received by the British Government. The Ministry now perceived that the Syndicate had not waged war; it had been simply exhibiting the uselessness of war as at present waged. Who now could deny that it would be folly to oppose the resources of ordinary warfare to those of what might be called prohibitive warfare.

Another idea arose in the minds of the wisest British statesmen. If prohibitive warfare were a good thing for America, it would be an equally good thing for England. More than that, it would be a better thing if only these two countries possessed the power of waging prohibitive warfare.

In three days a convention of peace was concluded between Great Britain and the American Syndicate acting for the United States, its provisions being made subject to such future treaties and alliances as the governments of the two nations might make with each other. In six days after the affair at Caerdaff, a committee of the American War Syndicate was in London, making arrangements, under the favourable auspices of the British Government, for the formation of an Anglo-American Syndicate of War.

The Atlantic Ocean now sprang into new life. It seemed impossible to imagine whence had come the multitude of vessels which now steamed and sailed upon its surface. Among these, going westward, were six crabs, and the spring-armoured vessel, once the Tallapoosa, going home to a triumphant reception, such as had never before been accorded to any vessel, whether of war or peace.

The blockade of the Canadian port, which had been effectively maintained without incident, was now raised, and the Syndicate's vessels proceeded to an American port.

The British ironclad, Adamant, at the conclusion of peace was still in tow of Crab C, and off the coast of Florida. A vessel was sent down the coast by the Syndicate to notify Crab C of what had occurred, and to order it to tow the Adamant to the Bermudas, and there deliver her to the British authorities. The vessel sent by the Syndicate, which was a fast coast-steamer, had scarcely hove in sight of the objects of her search when she was saluted by a ten-inch shell from the Adamant, followed almost immediately by two others. The commander of the Adamant had no idea that the war was at an end, and had never failed, during his involuntary cruise, to fire at anything which bore the American flag, or looked like an American craft.

Fortunately the coast steamer was not struck, and at the top of her speed retired to a greater distance, whence the Syndicate officer on board communicated with the crab by smoke signals.

During the time in which Crab C had had charge of the Adamant no communication had taken place between the two vessels. Whenever an air-pipe had been elevated for the purpose of using therein a speaking-tube, a volley from a machine-gun on the Adamant was poured upon it, and after several pipes had been shot away the director of the crab ceased his efforts to confer with those on the ironclad. It had been necessary to place the outlets of the ventilating apparatus of the crab under the forward ends of some of the upper roof-plates.

When Crab C had received her orders, she put about the prow of the great warship, and proceeded to tow her north-eastward, the commander of the Adamant taking a parting crack with his heaviest stern-gun at the vessel which had brought the order for his release.

All the way from the American coast to the Bermuda Islands, the great Adamant blazed, thundered, and roared, not only because her commander saw, or fancied he saw, an American vessel, but to notify all crabs, repellers, and any other vile invention of the enemy that may have been recently put forth to blemish the sacred surface of the sea, that the Adamant still floated, with the heaviest coat of mail and the finest and most complete armament in the world, ready to sink anything hostile which came near enough—but not too near.

When the commander found that he was bound for the Bermudas, he did not understand it, unless, indeed, those islands had been captured by the enemy. But he did not stop firing. Indeed, should he find the Bermudas under the American flag, he would fire at that flag and whatever carried it, as long as a shot or a shell or a charge of powder remained to him.

But when he reached British waters, and slowly entering St. George's harbour, saw around him the British flag floating as proudly as it floated above his own great ship, he confessed himself utterly bewildered; but he ordered the men at every gun to stand by their piece until he was boarded by a boat from the fort, and informed of the true state of affairs.

But even then, when weary Crab C raised herself from her fighting depth, and steamed to a dock, the commander of the Adamant could scarcely refrain from sending a couple of tons of iron into the beastly sea-devil which had had the impertinence to tow him about against his will.

No time was lost by the respective Governments of Great Britain and the United States in ratifying the peace made through the Syndicate, and in concluding a military and naval alliance, the basis of which should be the use by these two nations, and by no other nations, of the instantaneous motor. The treaty was made and adopted with much more despatch than generally accompanies such agreements between nations, for both Governments felt the importance of placing themselves, without delay, in that position from which, by means of their united control of paramount methods of warfare, they might become the arbiters of peace.

The desire to evolve that power which should render opposition useless had long led men from one warlike invention to another. Every one who had constructed a new kind of gun, a new kind of armour, or a new explosive, thought that he had

Frank R. Stockton

solved the problem, or was on his way to do so. The inventor of the instantaneous motor had done it.

The treaty provided that all subjects concerning hostilities between either or both of the contracting powers and other nations should be referred to a Joint High Commission, appointed by the two powers; and if war should be considered necessary, it should be prosecuted and conducted by the Anglo-American War Syndicate, within limitations prescribed by the High Commission.

The contract made with the new Syndicate was of the most stringent order, and contained every provision that ingenuity or foresight of man could invent or suggest to make it impossible for the Syndicate to transfer to any other nation the use of the instantaneous motor.

Throughout all classes in sympathy with the Administrative parties of Great Britain and the United States there was a feeling of jubilant elation on account of the alliance and the adoption by the two nations of the means of prohibitive warfare. This public sentiment acted even upon the opposition; and the majority of army and navy officers in the two countries felt bound to admit that the arts of war in which they had been educated were things of the past. Of course there were members of the army and navy in both countries who deprecated the new state of things. But there were also men, still living, who deprecated the abolition of the old wooden seventy-four gun ship.

A British artillery officer conversing with a member of the American Syndicate at a London club, said to him:—

"Do you know that you made a great mistake in the beginning of your operations with the motor-guns? If you had contrived an attachment to the motor which should have made an infernal thunder-clap and a storm of smoke at the moment of discharge it would have saved you a lot of money and time and trouble. The work of the motor on the Canadian coast was terrible enough, but people could see no connection between that and the guns on your vessels. If you could have sooner shown that connection you might have saved yourselves the trouble of crossing the Atlantic. And, to prove this, one of the most satisfactory points connected with your work on the Welsh coast was the jet of smoke which came from the repeller every time she discharged a motor. If it had not been for those jets, I believe there would be people now in the opposition who would swear that Caerdaff had been mined, and that the Ministry were a party to it."

"Your point is well taken," said the American, "and should it ever be necessary to discharge any more bombs,—which I hope it may not be,—we shall take care to show a visible and audible connection between cause and effect."

"The devil take it, sir!" cried an old captain of an English ship-of-the-line, who was sitting near by. "What you are talking about is not war! We might as well send out a Codfish Trust to settle national disputes. In the next sea-fight we'll save ourselves the trouble of gnawing and crunching at the sterns of the enemy. We'll simply send a note aboard requesting the foreigner to be so good as to send us his rudder by bearer, which, if properly marked and numbered, will be returned to him on the conclusion of peace. This would do just as well as twisting it off, and save expense. No, sir, I will not join you in a julep! *I* have made no alliance over new-fangled inventions! Waiter, fetch me some rum and hot water!"

In the midst of the profound satisfaction with which the members of the American War Syndicate regarded the success of their labours,—labours alike profitable to themselves and to the recently contending nations,—and in the gratified pride with which they received the popular and official congratulations which were showered upon them, there was but one little cloud, one regret.

In the course of the great Syndicate War a life had been lost. Thomas Hutchins, while assisting in the loading of coal on one of the repellers, was accidentally killed by the falling of a derrick.

The Syndicate gave a generous sum to the family of the unfortunate man, and throughout the United States the occurrence occasioned a deep feeling of sympathetic regret. A popular subscription was started to build a monument to the memory of Hutchins, and contributions came, not only from all parts of the United States, but from many persons in Great Britain who wished to assist in the erection of this tribute to the man who had fallen in the contest which had been of as much benefit to their country as to his own.

Some weeks after the conclusion of the treaty, a public question was raised, which at first threatened to annoy the American Government; but it proved to be of little moment. An anti-Administration paper in Peakville, Arkansas, asserted that in the whole of the published treaty there was not one word in regard to the fisheries question, the complications arising from which had been the cause of the war. Other papers took up the matter, and the Government then discovered that in drawing up the treaty the fisheries business had been entirely overlooked. There was a good deal of surprise in official circles when this discovery was announced; but as it was considered that the fisheries question was one which would take care of itself, or be readily disposed of in connection with a number of other minor points which remained to be settled between the two countries, it was decided to take no notice of the implied charge of neglect, and to let the matter drop. And as the opposition party took no real interest in the question, but little more was said about it.

Both countries were too well satisfied with the general result to waste time or discussion over small matters. Great Britain had lost some forts and some ships; but these would have been comparatively useless in the new system of warfare. On the other hand, she had gained, not only the incalculable advantage of the alliance, but a magnificent and unsurpassed landlocked basin on the coast of Wales.

The United States had been obliged to pay an immense sum on account of the contract with the War Syndicate, but this was considered money so well spent, and so much less than an ordinary war would have cost, that only the most violent anti-Administration journals ever alluded to it.

Reduction of military and naval forces, and gradual disarmament, was now the policy of the allied nations. Such forces and such vessels as might be demanded for the future operations of the War Syndicate were retained. A few field batteries of motor-guns were all that would be needed on land, and a comparatively small number of armoured ships would suffice to carry the motor-guns that would be required at sea.

Now there would be no more mere exhibitions of the powers of the instantaneous motor-bomb. Hereafter, if battles must be fought, they would be battles of annihilation.

This is the history of the Great Syndicate War. Whether or not the Anglo-American Syndicate was ever called upon to make war, it is not to be stated here. But certain it is that after the formation of this Syndicate all the nations of the world began to teach English in their schools, and the Spirit of Civilization raised her head with a confident smile.

Frank R. Stockton

ABOUT THE AUTHOR

 **Frank R. Stockton** (April 5, 1834 - April 20, 1902), was an American writer and humorist, best known today for a series of innovative children's fairy tales that were widely popular during the last decades of the 19th century. Stockton avoided the didactic moralizing common to children's stories of the time, instead using clever humor to poke at greed, violence, abuse of power and other human foibles, describing his fantastic characters' adventures in a charming, matter-of-fact way in stories like "The Griffin and the Minor Canon" (1885) and "The Bee-Man of Orn" (1887), which was republished in 1964 in an edition illustrated by Maurice Sendak.

Born in Philadelphia, Stockton was the son of a prominent Methodist minister who discouraged him from a writing career. He supported himself as a wood engraver until his father's death in 1860; in 1867, he moved back to Philadelphia to write for a newspaper founded by his brother. His first fairy tale, "Ting-a-ling," was published that year in The Riverside Magazine; his first book collection appeared in 1870.

He died of a cerebral hemorrhage in 1902. His collected works, 23 volumes of stories for adults and children, were published between 1899 and 1904.

Choose from Thousands of 1stWorldLibrary Classics By

A. M. Barnard	Booth Tarkington	Edward Everett Hale
Ada Leverson	Boyd Cable	Edward J. O'Biren
Adolphus William Ward	Bram Stoker	Edward S. Ellis
Aesop	C. Collodi	Edwin L. Arnold
Agatha Christie	C. E. Orr	Eleanor Atkins
Alexander Aaronsohn	C. M. Ingleby	Eleanor Hallowell Abbott
Alexander Kielland	Carolyn Wells	Eliot Gregory
Alexandre Dumas	Catherine Parr Traill	Elizabeth Gaskell
Alfred Gatty	Charles A. Eastman	Elizabeth McCracken
Alfred Ollivant	Charles Amory Beach	Elizabeth Von Arnim
Alice Duer Miller	Charles Dickens	Ellem Key
Alice Turner Curtis	Charles Dudley Warner	Emerson Hough
Alice Dunbar	Charles Farrar Browne	Emilie F. Carlen
Allen Chapman	Charles Ives	Emily Bronte
Alleyne Ireland	Charles Kingsley	Emily Dickinson
Ambrose Bierce	Charles Klein	Enid Bagnold
Amelia E. Barr	Charles Hanson Towne	Enilor Macartney Lane
Amory H. Bradford	Charles Lathrop Pack	Erasmus W. Jones
Andrew Lang	Charles Romyn Dake	Ernie Howard Pie
Andrew McFarland Davis	Charles Whibley	Ethel May Dell
Andy Adams	Charles Willing Beale	Ethel Turner
Angela Brazil	Charlotte M. Braeme	Ethel Watts Mumford
Anna Alice Chapin	Charlotte M. Yonge	Eugene Sue
Anna Sewell	Charlotte Perkins Stetson	Eugenie Foa
Annie Besant	Clair W. Hayes	Eugene Wood
Annie Hamilton Donnell	Clarence Day Jr.	Eustace Hale Ball
Annie Payson Call	Clarence E. Mulford	Evelyn Everett-green
Annie Roe Carr	Clemence Housman	Everard Cotes
Annonaymous	Confucius	F. H. Cheley
Anton Chekhov	Coningsby Dawson	F. J. Cross
Archibald Lee Fletcher	Cornelis DeWitt Wilcox	F. Marion Crawford
Arnold Bennett	Cyril Burleigh	Fannie E. Newberry
Arthur C. Benson	D. H. Lawrence	Federick Austin Ogg
Arthur Conan Doyle	Daniel Defoe	Ferdinand Ossendowski
Arthur M. Winfield	David Garnett	Fergus Hume
Arthur Ransome	Dinah Craik	Florence A. Kilpatrick
Arthur Schnitzler	Don Carlos Janes	Fremont B. Deering
Arthur Train	Donald Keyhoe	Francis Bacon
Atticus	Dorothy Kilner	Francis Darwin
B.H. Baden-Powell	Dougan Clark	Frances Hodgson Burnett
B. M. Bower	Douglas Fairbanks	Frances Parkinson Keyes
B. C. Chatterjee	E. Nesbit	Frank Gee Patchin
Baroness Emmuska Orczy	E. P. Roe	Frank Harris
Baroness Orczy	E. Phillips Oppenheim	Frank Jewett Mather
Basil King	E. S. Brooks	Frank L. Packard
Bayard Taylor	Earl Barnes	Frank V. Webster
Ben Macomber	Edgar Rice Burroughs	Frederic Stewart Isham
Bertha Muzzy Bower	Edith Van Dyne	Frederick Trevor Hill
Bjornstjerne Bjornson	Edith Wharton	Frederick Winslow Taylor

Friedrich Kerst
Friedrich Nietzsche
Fyodor Dostoyevsky
G.A. Henty
G.K. Chesterton
Gabrielle E. Jackson
Garrett P. Serviss
Gaston Leroux
George A. Warren
George Ade
Geroge Bernard Shaw
George Cary Eggleston
George Durston
George Ebers
George Eliot
George Gissing
George MacDonald
George Meredith
George Orwell
George Sylvester Viereck
George Tucker
George W. Cable
George Wharton James
Gertrude Atherton
Gordon Casserly
Grace E. King
Grace Gallatin
Grace Greenwood
Grant Allen
Guillermo A. Sherwell
Gulielma Zollinger
Gustav Flaubert
H. A. Cody
H. B. Irving
H.C. Bailey
H. G. Wells
H. H. Munro
H. Irving Hancock
H. R. Naylor
H. Rider Haggard
H. W. C. Davis
Haldeman Julius
Hall Caine
Hamilton Wright Mabie
Hans Christian Andersen
Harold Avery
Harold McGrath
Harriet Beecher Stowe
Harry Castlemon
Harry Coghill
Harry Houidini

Hayden Carruth
Helent Hunt Jackson
Helen Nicolay
Hendrik Conscience
Hendy David Thoreau
Henri Barbusse
Henrik Ibsen
Henry Adams
Henry Ford
Henry Frost
Henry James
Henry Jones Ford
Henry Seton Merriman
Henry W Longfellow
Herbert A. Giles
Herbert Carter
Herbert N. Casson
Herman Hesse
Hildegard G. Frey
Homer
Honore De Balzac
Horace B. Day
Horace Walpole
Horatio Alger Jr.
Howard Pyle
Howard R. Garis
Hugh Lofting
Hugh Walpole
Humphry Ward
Ian Maclaren
Inez Haynes Gillmore
Irving Bacheller
Isabel Cecilia Williams
Isabel Hornibrook
Israel Abrahams
Ivan Turgenev
J.G.Austin
J. Henri Fabre
J. M. Barrie
J. M. Walsh
J. Macdonald Oxley
J. R. Miller
J. S. Fletcher
J. S. Knowles
J. Storer Clouston
J. W. Duffield
Jack London
Jacob Abbott
James Allen
James Andrews
James Baldwin

James Branch Cabell
James DeMille
James Joyce
James Lane Allen
James Lane Allen
James Oliver Curwood
James Oppenheim
James Otis
James R. Driscoll
Jane Abbott
Jane Austen
Jane L. Stewart
Janet Aldridge
Jens Peter Jacobsen
Jerome K. Jerome
Jessie Graham Flower
John Buchan
John Burroughs
John Cournos
John F. Kennedy
John Gay
John Glasworthy
John Habberton
John Joy Bell
John Kendrick Bangs
John Milton
John Philip Sousa
John Taintor Foote
Jonas Lauritz Idemil Lie
Jonathan Swift
Joseph A. Altsheler
Joseph Carey
Joseph Conrad
Joseph E. Badger Jr
Joseph Hergesheimer
Joseph Jacobs
Jules Vernes
Julian Hawthrone
Julie A Lippmann
Justin Huntly McCarthy
Kakuzo Okakura
Karle Wilson Baker
Kate Chopin
Kenneth Grahame
Kenneth McGaffey
Kate Langley Bosher
Kate Langley Bosher
Katherine Cecil Thurston
Katherine Stokes
L. A. Abbot
L. T. Meade

L. Frank Baum
Latta Griswold
Laura Dent Crane
Laura Lee Hope
Laurence Housman
Lawrence Beasley
Leo Tolstoy
Leonid Andreyev
Lewis Carroll
Lewis Sperry Chafer
Lilian Bell
Lloyd Osbourne
Louis Hughes
Louis Joseph Vance
Louis Tracy
Louisa May Alcott
Lucy Fitch Perkins
Lucy Maud Montgomery
Luther Benson
Lydia Miller Middleton
Lyndon Orr
M. Corvus
M. H. Adams
Margaret E. Sangster
Margret Howth
Margaret Vandercook
Margaret W. Hungerford
Margret Penrose
Maria Edgeworth
Maria Thompson Daviess
Mariano Azuela
Marion Polk Angellotti
Mark Overton
Mark Twain
Mary Austin
Mary Catherine Crowley
Mary Cole
Mary Hastings Bradley
Mary Roberts Rinehart
Mary Rowlandson
M. Wollstonecraft Shelley
Maud Lindsay
Max Beerbohm
Myra Kelly
Nathaniel Hawthrone
Nicolo Machiavelli
O. F. Walton
Oscar Wilde

Owen Johnson
P.G. Wodehouse
Paul and Mabel Thorne
Paul G. Tomlinson
Paul Severing
Percy Brebner
Percy Keese Fitzhugh
Peter B. Kyne
Plato
Quincy Allen
R. Derby Holmes
R. L. Stevenson
R. S. Ball
Rabindranath Tagore
Rahul Alvares
Ralph Bonehill
Ralph Henry Barbour
Ralph Victor
Ralph Waldo Emmerson
Rene Descartes
Ray Cummings
Rex Beach
Rex E. Beach
Richard Harding Davis
Richard Jefferies
Richard Le Gallienne
Robert Barr
Robert Frost
Robert Gordon Anderson
Robert L. Drake
Robert Lansing
Robert Lynd
Robert Michael Ballantyne
Robert W. Chambers
Rosa Nouchette Carey
Rudyard Kipling
Saint Augustine
Samuel B. Allison
Samuel Hopkins Adams
Sarah Bernhardt
Sarah C. Hallowell
Selma Lagerlof
Sherwood Anderson
Sigmund Freud
Standish O'Grady
Stanley Weyman
Stella Benson
Stella M. Francis

Stephen Crane
Stewart Edward White
Stijn Streuvels
Swami Abhedananda
Swami Parmananda
T. S. Ackland
T. S. Arthur
The Princess Der Ling
Thomas A. Janvier
Thomas A Kempis
Thomas Anderton
Thomas Bailey Aldrich
Thomas Bulfinch
Thomas De Quincey
Thomas Dixon
Thomas H. Huxley
Thomas Hardy
Thomas More
Thornton W. Burgess
U. S. Grant
Upton Sinclair
Valentine Williams
Various Authors
Vaughan Kester
Victor Appleton
Victor G. Durham
Victoria Cross
Virginia Woolf
Wadsworth Camp
Walter Camp
Walter Scott
Washington Irving
Wilbur Lawton
Wilkie Collins
Willa Cather
Willard F. Baker
William Dean Howells
William le Queux
W. Makepeace Thackeray
William W. Walter
William Shakespeare
Winston Churchill
Yei Theodora Ozaki
Yogi Ramacharaka
Young E. Allison
Zane Grey